UP ABOVE THE WORLD

Ecco Press Books by Paul Bowles

The Delicate Prey (STORIES)

A Distant Episode (STORIES)

Jean Genet in Tangier by Mohamed Choukri
(TRANSLATION)

Points in Time (FICTION)

Their Heads Are Green and Their Hands Are Blue
(ESSAYS)

Up Above the World (NOVEL)

Without Stopping (AUTOBIOGRAPHY)

About Paul Bowles

An Invisible Spectator
by Christopher Sawyer-Lauçanno
(BIOGRAPHY)

UP ABOVE THE WORLD

PAUL BOWLES

THE ECCO PRESS

First published by The Ecco Press in 1982
100 West Broad Street, Hopewell, NJ 08525
Published simultaneously in Canada
by Penguin Books Canada, Ltd., Ontario
Printed in the United States of America
The Ecco Press logo by Ahmed Yacoubi

Library of Congress Cataloging in Publication Data

Bowles, Paul Frederic, 1911–
    Up above the world.
    (Neglected books of the 20th century)
    Reprint. Originally published: London: Owen, 1967.
    I. Title.
PS3552.0874U6   1982   813´.54   82-2357
ISBN 0-88001-302-8 (pbk.)   AACR2

Fourth Printing, 1992

ONE

1

THE SLADES SAT DOWN to their breakfast more asleep than awake. The ship was in; they had heard its mournful whistle when it had arrived out in the harbor at some dark hour during the night. Now it was only a question of getting aboard with the luggage. Last night, when they returned from their pre-bedtime walk around the deserted town, the proprietor had told them to set their minds at rest: the night watchman would wake them at half past five, and breakfast would be served in the dining room at six. It was now twenty to seven. In the center of the room a black woman on her knees scrubbed the already spotless board floor. There was no one else in evidence, although faint sounds came from the region of the kitchen. Someone, they assumed, was making the coffee that would finally persuade them they were alive. The table had not been cleared away after last night's meal; at each place lay a half-eaten custard.

"I'll kill myself if we miss it," she declared.

"Oh, God." Then as if correcting himself, he said, "We won't miss it."

Outside the window the morning mist dripped from banana leaf to banana leaf. The clock over the sideboard ticked fast and loud. Time bomb, Dr. Slade thought as he looked out over the wet greenness of the hotel gardens.

"Just don't get nervous," he said, yawning. "We've got plenty of time." There was a difference between an ordinary relaxed yawn and this tight trembling one that came up convulsively from the bottom of his stomach. He counted to ten and jumped up.

"Where the *hell* is that coffee?" he cried in a sudden fury, wheeling in search of a door to the kitchen. A heavy red-faced woman was coming into the dining room; as he approached her he was aware of her bright cheeks, and he wondered fleetingly if she would be the wife of the proprietor. His *Buenos días* was a mutter, but she was already greeting him in English, and with a broad smile. He went on in the direction of the kitchen sounds and found the place, a dark cavern where a sleepy Negro fanned a smoking wood fire in a stove. "*Café! Café!*" cried Dr. Slade.

The man pointed to the garden, and Dr. Slade stepped out through the doorway onto the coarse sand. Poinsettia bushes grew under the young papaya trees; the flowers looked like wet red tissue paper. He went back into the dining room through a side door, cursing, and saw the steam rising from the two cups of coffee on the table. Mrs. Slade was no longer in the room.

The prospect of drinking the coffee while it was still hot, even with its usual complement of condensed milk, was too tempting to be disregarded. He sat down. "I trust that was a useful trip," he would say when she came back. Or, "Your digestion's important too, you know." A dog was barking furiously in the street just outside the window, and excited voices called. "When you're really pressed for time, there's an art in making each second count. You merely fit each thing you've got to do into the right bit of time." A girl appeared with a plate of bread.

"*Hay mantequilla?*" he asked her. She stared at him, shrugged her shoulders, and said she would go and see. He called after her to bring another cup of coffee, and glanced at the clock: twelve minutes to seven.

There was the sound of heel-taps behind him, approaching quickly from the hall. Mrs. Slade was at the table before he could put down his cup and turn. There was an expression of amused preoccupation on her face as she seated herself.

"Terribly funny," she said, more to herself than to him, and then she sipped her coffee while he waited for an explanation. The girl returned without the butter, but with two plates of ham and eggs. Before he began to eat, he said, "What?"

Mrs. Slade seemed not to have heard him, and plunged into her food with gusto.

2

THE DOCK WAS AT THE END of the street; from there they could see the ship, huge and unmoving in the center of the circular bay. A motor launch with a green canopy crossed and recrossed the bright water between the dock and the vessel while they stood waiting to get into the customs shed.

"It's going to be a nice day, after all," Dr. Slade announced with satisfaction. "That fog was just decoration." He set his briefcase down so that it leaned against his leg.

"It'd be just like them to pull up the anchor and start off while we stand here waiting," Mrs. Slade said grimly.

Dr. Slade laughed. Had such a thing really happened, he would have minded it even more than she, but in his experience the world was a rational place. "I only hope they can make frozen daiquiris," he said; it was a remark which might momentarily set her mind at rest.

The little motor launch chugged up to the dock, and out of it climbed the big woman with the pink cheeks, her wide forehead glistening with sweat. In her hand she held some papers which she waved at the two uniformed men standing nearby; they pointed to the customs shed.

"Look at Mrs. Crazy," said Dr. Slade with interest. "Isn't she something? She's already been out to the ship and back."

"She forgot her letter of credit." said Mrs. Slade.

Dr. Slade looked at his wife. "How do you know that?"

"She told me. She's a passenger. They won't honor the letter of credit on the ship, and she thinks if she can find a bank she may be able to get hold of some money. It's a whole saga. I lent her ten dollars."

"You lent *her money?*" cried Dr. Slade, scandalized. Then hearing his voice, he tried to alter its tone, and with discernibly false gentleness continued, "What for?"

"She'll give it back, dear." Mrs. Slade's voice was one calculated to calm a small child.

The woman was approaching them, panting. Dr. Slade had the time only to whisper, "That's not the point."

"Don't you let the ship go off without me!" she cried, shaking her black leather handbag at them playfully.

Mrs. Slade smiled. "Oh, I think you have time."

"I hope so," said Dr. Slade, not quite *sotto voce*. His inflection made it sound as if he had said "I hope not."

"Tell them they've *got* to wait," she called over her shoulder.

"Ridiculous," said Dr. Slade.

"I think she's rather touching," Mrs. Slade murmured pensively, looking after the retreating figure.

Dr. Slade did not reply. He stared out across the still harbor, and there came to him the idea that it was sometimes possible for two people who were close to one another to be very separate indeed. His eye followed the fuzzy line of forested mountains above the landlocked harbor, and the word *touching* took on an unaccustomed, disturbing dimension for him as he pursued the course of his thought.

3

THE COASTWISE JOURNEY FROM LA RESACA to Puerto Farol took only a day and a half, but Mrs. Slade, being uncertain which articles were in which valises, had found it necessary to unpack everything. Aware that he was not going to be able to prevent the operation, Dr. Slade had retired to the library to avoid having to witness it. Later in the afternoon he went in search of her and found her, shining with sun oil, prostrate on a deck mattress by the pool. He knelt proudly beside her, conscious of the other sunbathers' interest.

"How're you weathering lap two?" he asked her.

"What?" She squinted up at him.

"The second lap of the Slade Anniversary Expedition."

"Oh." She stretched with pleasure and waited a while before saying, "I meant to tell you. We're having drinks with Mrs. Rainmantle at six. Down in the bar."

He was mystified. "What for?" he asked, but his wife merely looked at him.

"You don't have to come," she told him.

He stood up. "Don't I?"

He walked slowly back to the stern of the ship and stood looking over the rail down into the soapy wake below. Along the horizon distant cumulus clouds leaned in a row like crooked pillars. Suddenly he felt very much alone. He stared for a long time at the far-off slanting cloud-towers. Before coming on the trip, during his medical checkup, he had forced himself to refer to the subject. "She could be my daughter. Or even my granddaughter, for that matter." The other physician had laughed. "Won't hurt to keep it in mind," he said.

He began to walk again, finally, and took the first stairway he found up to the boat deck, where he went eight times around.

Mrs. Rainmantle was already in the bar when they got there, seated on a high stool, wearing the same loosely fitting gray silk suit. Her hair was matted and stiff. Pretty bad, thought Dr. Slade; he would have liked to take out his handkerchief and wipe the grease and sweat from her forehead. It was something that required attention, like a child whose nose needs blowing.

When they had their planter's punches safely set on a table in the corner, he rubbed a drop of water from his lapel and said to Mrs. Rainmantle, "Was the bank obliging?" He saw the furious glance his wife darted in his direction.

"Oh, no! It was a completely useless trip," she replied airily.

"You mean it was shut?" said Dr. Slade, narrowing his eyes as he looked at her. He was aware of a whole series of tiny agitated movements being gone through by his wife in her attempt to catch his eye, but he would not look at her.

Smiling vaguely, Mrs. Rainmantle took a large gulp of her drink.

"It was open, all right. But they wouldn't help me."

"What?" he exclaimed. "I should think if you'd contacted your consul he might have done something." (Although would he? he thought. Perhaps not, if he took a good look at you.)

"I saw him," she explained. "He was perfectly pleasant. But he didn't feel he could take the responsibility. I didn't have the identification card with me. I showed him my passport and letters . . ." Her voice died as she recalled the details in the scene of her failure.

To his relief Mrs. Slade laughed. Good girl! he thought, daring to hope that her annoyance with him would now be mitigated. But even as she was laughing, she glanced at him, and he recognized his error.

They had another round of drinks. While they were talking, Mrs. Rainmantle drew the steward aside and had signed the chit before either of them was aware of what was happening. "Of course I invited you," she announced regally, and succeeded in silencing them both.

She rose. "I'm going to have one of those wonderful hot salt baths. See you anon."

"Ah," said Dr. Slade. When she was gone, he sat down. "It still wasn't ten dollars."

After dinner they wandered along the promenade deck; there was a warm wind and a bright moon. "How can you say I was rude?" he cried. "Is there any reason why I should go out of my way to treat that woman with kid gloves?"

She had her hands on the railing and was looking out across the shimmering expanse of moonlit water. "Yes! Yes!" she said, in a low but passionate voice. "There is! I always make an effort with your friends."

17

"Friends! Yes, but is she a friend?"

"You saw I was on friendly terms with her."

He was silent a moment while he thought, I'm making too much of it. "How did we get into all this?" he said. Then he laughed, caught hold of her hand, and pulled her away from the railing. They started to walk.

"It won't happen again," he told her. Still holding her hand, he pressed it as he spoke. Later, while they were dancing, he remained on the lookout for Mrs. Rainmantle, to be more certain of being able to avoid her, but she was not among the guests in the Bahia Bar.

A very fine rain was falling as the ship pushed into the harbor of Puerto Farol. It dimmed the steep outlines of the mountains that climbed upward to disappear in the enormous heavy sky. Even before the anchor had been cast, Dr. Slade heard the calling of countless frogs from the land. A shore excursion had been arranged for the passengers who were interested in visiting the stelae of San Ignacio.

"Is there anything as physically depressing as the sight of a lot of people together in one place?" said Mrs. Slade. "Thank God, we're leaving this ark." They stood by the rail, looking toward the land; a slight backward toss of her head indicated the passengers behind them.

"Are there sharks in the water, Daddy?" A small girl with pigtails standing beside Dr. Slade pointed downward. "Daddy, are there?" No one paid her any attention, and so Dr. Slade said to her in a matter-of-fact voice, "Of course there are, dear."

"Don't you believe him, honey," Mrs. Slade told her. "He's just teasing."

Dr. Slade laughed. "You fall in and see what happens,"

he said. The child looked from one of them to the other and backed away from the railing.

"Why are you so mean?" demanded Mrs. Slade. "Why do you want to frighten the poor little thing?"

Dr. Slade was impatient. "She asked for information and she got it," he said with finality. Through his binoculars he was scanning the seaside forest of coconut palms ahead. He had just caught sight of Mrs. Rainmantle coming along the deck, and he hoped to avoid having to greet her. Above all, he wanted not to go ashore in the same launch with her. Out of the corner of his eye, while he pretended to be looking through the glasses, he saw her work her way through the crowd to the rail farther astern, and was relieved.

4

THEY STOOD AT THE DESK in the front hall of the hotel, listening to the wide sound of the rain that fell; it came down heavily now. The man behind the desk was eating a mango. Short strings of the fruit's pulp had got caught in his bushy mustache and hung from the hairs like tiny yellow worms above his lip. "*Pues sí, señores,*" he resumed, without wiping his face, "The train for the capital leaves every morning at half past six. But there are many things to see here in Puerto Farol."

Dr. Slade looked out of the doorway across the veranda with its broken wicker furniture, past the waterfall of rain that splattered down from the door, to the empty garden beyond. A large buzzard suddenly appeared and settled clumsily on the bare plank that was the veranda's railing. For a moment he thought it was going to topple over. Like a mass of charred newspaper it wavered there for an instant, then steadied itself, folded its wings and let its raw red head fall to one side on its breast.

The man picked his nose with his forefinger now as he spoke. "There is a place called Paraíso only thirty-two kilometers from here. There are the ruins of San Ignacio. Very interesting. Big stones in the jungle, with faces in them. They'll give you nightmares!" His laugh broke into a cough, and he spat straight down from where he stood, watching the mass of sputum fall to the floor. Then he seemed to be doing a little dance by himself behind the desk as he scuffed it with the sole of his shoe. "*Sabe lo que son, las pesadillas?*"

"Yes, yes, of course," said Dr. Slade. "We'll be taking the train tomorrow morning, and we'll need at least three men to help with our luggage. I just wanted to let you know now."

"It's fantastic!" Mrs. Slade exclaimed, looking up at her husband. "A town as big as this without a single taxi!"

"A town as big as this with only this one hotel," he retorted. "The walk's nothing. Fifteen minutes. But God, we've got to sleep here. And we've got to eat here. The taxi's the least of my worries."

The man behind the desk was tearing the skin from another mango; the tart varnish-like odor filled the hall. Mrs. Slade spoke very little Spanish. "*Mango bueno?*" she said to the man.

"*Regular,*" he answered without looking up.

They wandered out onto the veranda; the buzzard did

20

nct move. The air smelled of flowers, and there was a constant tapestry of insect sounds audible behind the roar of the rain. They sat down in two worn wicker rocking chairs and stared out at the blinding watery gray noon. From time to time there was the very loud sound of a rooster crowing from somewhere nearby.

"I think I'll change before lunch. I feel wet and dirty," said Mrs. Slade.

"At least we got the good room," Dr. Slade replied with satisfaction.

Mrs. Slade laughed derisively; he supposed it was the idea of using the word *good*. "It's going to be rice and beans, I can tell you," he said. "But you like that, of course." He looked at her with indulgence.

"I'm so lucky!" She smiled and rocked a bit; the chair creaked dangerously.

Around the edge of the empty plaza, avoiding the deeper puddles, moved a small car; it came to a stop in front of them, at the foot of the veranda steps. The buzzard on the railing flopped down out of sight, the car door opened, and Dr. Slade saw what he immediately told himself he had expected to see: the red face and high gray coiffure of Mrs. Rainmantle emerging from the little sedan. She nodded her head to the driver, slammed the door, and hurried up the steps, panting and wet. When she recognized the Slades sitting there in front of her, her preoccupied expression altered to one of astonishment and pleasure. Dr. Slade rose slowly and extended his hand.

"Don't tell me you missed all *three* of the buses to San Ignacio!" she cried. "May I?" She dropped into his chair. He looked down at her apathetically, half hoping to see the chair collapse under her weight, but it was decep-

21

tively resistant. "Oh, of course. I forgot. You're disembarking here, too, aren't you?" She squeezed her hair with both hands, and rivulets of rain ran down her face.

"You're wet through to the skin," observed Mrs. Slade.

She laughed. "To the bone, I think."

Mrs. Slade watched the car making its way through the mud on the opposite side of the public garden. "Was that a taxi you had?" she asked suddenly.

"That was the British consul. More trouble. Now they won't let me take my luggage off the ship. I have a bar bill. But don't let me get started on it."

"Hah!" said Dr. Slade, who was walking slowly back and forth in front of the two women.

"It sounds very strange to me," Mrs. Slade said cautiously. Then she added, "You're getting off the ship here at Puerto Farol, then?"

Mrs. Rainmantle laughed. "Of course I'll get off all right. The consul is going to take care of it the first thing this afternoon. If only my son had been able to meet me. . . . So unnecessary." She sneezed violently.

Mrs. Slade stood up. "You're wet and you have nothing to change into. That can't *be*."

"I know. It's an impossible situation."

"I was wondering . . ." Mrs. Slade looked doubtful.

"Mercy!" laughed Mrs. Rainmantle. "A little thing like you, with your waist? Never in the world! You couldn't possibly have anything."

Mrs. Slade hesitated another instant. "No," she said suddenly. "Come up with me. I've got something. Really."

At the end of a series of facetious protests, Mrs. Rainmantle let herself be led upstairs, and Dr. Slade sat down again in the rocking chair he had given her. The rain was lessening, and the mechanical sound of the insects in the trees came louder. He sat looking straight ahead. A skeletal and nearly furless cat crawled around the corner of the veranda and stretched out near his feet. Now and then he drummed with his fingers on the chair arm, and once he said aloud incredulously, in a voice heavy with disgust, "I'll be damned."

5

DR. SLADE WENT IN to lunch in a state of desperate boredom tempered with resentment; it had shaken him a little to see how bad luck could be prolonged to such unlikely lengths. Only three other passengers from the ship had finished their voyage at Puerto Farol. They were all in the dining room at the moment—three men sitting at three separate tables along the wall, watching the center, where the *turistas* sat. Here Mrs. Rainmantle, heavily made up now, and wearing Mrs. Slade's most baroque Japanese kimono, was dispensing bloody marys. She had ordered a large can of tomato juice from the refrigerator in the corner, and pulled a bottle of vodka from her handbag.

"I oughtn't to do this before lunch," she was saying. "But there are times when the call must be obeyed. And I feel the call."

"Well, I'm with you," Mrs. Slade told her. "Here's to you." She held up her glass. "May you arrive tomorrow night in the capital! Complete with luggage!"

Mrs. Rainmantle made a sad face. "I can't go to-morrow. I've got to see the consul again in the morning. I won't be able to leave until the *next* morning."

"What a shame!" said Dr. Slade. He could see from the expression on his wife's face that she was beginning to consider the possibility of delaying their own departure, and so he said firmly, "We're going tomorrow." Then, less certainly, "But we're bound to see you up there."

"I should think so!" agreed Mrs. Slade with warmth. "You'll call us at the hotel as soon as you have a minute."

Dr. Slade drank deeply from his glass and let their conversation flow over his head. Without listening, he perceived the outline of the story. A cockatoo in a back patio screamed twice; it was the voice of a demon. "Good God! We're back in the violent ward," said Mrs. Rainmantle.

By now he knew that she was a Canadian who lived in London and who was in the habit of coming here to visit her son. Still it was not necessary to listen: the high points of the story were so often reiterated that the graph was clear. He yawned and tapped his fingers on the table, looking out of the window at the wet leaves and tin roofs.

The three solitary diners had left the room and gone for their siestas. Now and then Dr. Slade glanced at his wife apprehensively to see if she resented his long silence, but she seemed not to mind. Occasionally she even sent him a sweet little smile, as though it were understood that he appreciated the extended monologue as much as she; with his answering smile he tried to project an expression of forbearance. Now the rain had ceased, the sun was blazing, and steam rose from the earth outside the window.

"I always try to see something worthwhile when I

24

come out to visit Grover." One year she had been to the lake district, one year to see the volcanoes near the southern border of the republic. Again she had come via Trinidad and Georgetown in order to go up the Mazaruni to Roraima.

The waiter came in to clear off the table. "Ask him if he hung the *señora's* clothes near the stove, darling," said Mrs. Slade.

He spoke with the waiter. "They're dry," he announced.

"Hurray!" cried Mrs. Rainmantle. "Now we can go out. I had visions of myself sitting inside all afternoon, waiting, while you two went out on the town."

"We wouldn't have gone off without you," said Mrs. Slade.

"Gone where?" Dr. Slade asked. His wife looked at him once, rose from the table, and followed Mrs. Rainmantle and the waiter into the kitchen. He remained sitting alone in the room, looking out at the shining day, and wondering what a single man's sex life would be like in Puerto Farol. A few sad sick whores near the railway station, most likely. No moonlit idyls under the palms while the surf rolled over the warm sand nearby. These people read no books. A town of corrugated iron, raw concrete and barbed wire. He had seen enough of it on his way from the dock to the hotel.

Mrs. Slade called to him from the kitchen door. "We're going upstairs. We'll be right down."

6

THE SINGLE WINDOW, next to the door, gave directly onto the veranda that encircled the whole second story. This balcony was the one pleasant spot to be found on the premises of the Gran Hotel de la Independencia. Over the years a great collection of potted tropical plants had been set on the floor along its railings; these had flourished, pushed forth fronds and spikes, extended creepers and branches, with the result that in places they constituted a veritable forest to be got through as one made one's way along the gallery. In some of the open spots there was a lone rocking chair of the same variety as those downstairs at the entrance. "The older sisters," Mrs. Slade had said as they passed by them a few minutes ago.

They lay on their beds now, partially undressed, with the netting prudently tucked under the mattresses, relaxing, absently exchanging half-thoughts across the no-man's-land between the beds. The hot dusk had closed down upon the town and swiftly sealed it off. Darkness here was tangible and intimate; it palpitated on all sides. There were the waves of flower and plant odors that drifted through the open window, the steady chorus of insects and tree frogs from the high vegetation beyond the veranda, the flashing on and off of the fireflies that moved high above their heads, just under the palmwood beams of the ceiling.

"If we want air we've got to leave the window open," said Dr. Slade.

"We certainly can't sleep with it shut. Under these nets?"

"It's safe enough. There must be a man on duty downstairs."

Presently she murmured, "It's like being in a tent."

"What's that?" he asked. Another minute and he might have dozed.

"This room." Her voice became more animated. "It's like being outdoors. Listen!"

After a moment he said, "Wonderful music for sleeping. I wish we didn't have to get up for dinner."

"Mmm," she answered uncertainly.

They were silent for a long time, as he fell into a series of light naps. Every few minutes he opened his eyes and then allowed himself to slip comfortably off again. She thought of what she would wear down to dinner, of the unbelievable dimness of the light in the room. Lack of light made everything more difficult. This was the sort of room where there could be spiders and one would not see them. She decided to unpack nothing and to put the same things back on, damp with sweat though they were. It was Puerto Farol that was at fault; anywhere else it would have struck her as an unsavory idea to dress in damp clothes.

All at once it was later, and people were approaching along the veranda outside the window.

"Taylor! What time is it?" she cried.

Dr. Slade moaned. She waited. Presently he said, "Ten after eight."

"You've been asleep a long time," she told him, as though it required forgiving.

He stretched voluptuously and yawned. There were several people on the balcony outside the door, and they were making a surprising amount of noise. Valises were dropped carelessly onto the bare board floor; then came the sound of their being slid along it. Several men were speaking in Spanish, and then unmistakably there was Mrs. Rainmantle's high voice mixed in with the others. "*Pero . . . pero . . .*" she seemed to be saying.

"Sounds as if she got her bags, all right," said Dr. Slade, sitting up. He opened the curtains of the net, got out of the bed quickly, and pulled the gap shut after him. Taking care to get into his slippers, he shuffled over to the window and stood there, watching. After a moment he came back to his wife's bed and said in a low voice, "They've put her in next door."

Mrs. Slade made a sharp "Shhhh!"

The porters' footsteps were still banging and shaking the veranda as they went on their way downstairs. He saw her sit up indignantly and try to catch his eye through the curtain of netting. She struggled into her kimono and pulled the net open, staring out at him, looking rumpled and angry, and, he thought, very desirable. He gave a pleased chuckle and said, "She can't hear, she can't hear. Believe me. Listen." He held up his hand for a second. "All those insects. It's a kind of soundproofing. Unless you're going to shout."

"I was afraid she might be outside the door."

Her clothes were not appreciably drier than when she had taken them off. It seemed to her they had an odor of rum about them. "I wonder if perspiration can smell of what you've drunk," she said.

"Absolutely."

She did not question the information. Using an atomizer filled with Tabac Blond, she set to work trying to neutralize the scent.

Dr. Slade waited, watching her. "The room's full of it," he observed aloud.

"I'm ready," she said.

They went out. He had a small flashlight in his hand

to help them through the bottlenecks of vegetation. "You're so clever to have brought that along," she told him.

Dinner was identical to lunch; they were alone in the nearly dark dining room. They got through the meal as quickly as possible, refusing coffee afterward. It was surprising that Mrs. Rainmantle had not come down.

"I'd like to take a little turn around the square before I go back into my box," said Dr. Slade.

"All right." Her voice lacked enthusiasm. "I'll probably have insomnia anyway."

"No, you won't." He stroked her arm.

"God, it's hot," she said, jumping up. "Let's go."

7

THEY HAD CHOSEN A NARROW, well-lighted alley to walk in rather than a street; suddenly they found themselves not among houses and trees, but on a boardwalk above a swamp. The street lights began again much farther ahead; here it was dark, and their footsteps banged loud on the boards. As they advanced, the frogs directly under them stopped calling, but on all sides the sound continued.

"Strange place," said Dr. Slade. Had he been alone, he would surely have turned back, but with his wife along that was harder to do. She would store away the memory of his action for use as ammunition some day in an unrelated context. "You were afraid, for instance, to cross that swamp at Puerto Farol. Of course you were quite right. I was just waiting to see how far you'd go. But you have to admit you *were* afraid, darling."

"Bats!" she exclaimed. "I saw some bats back there just before we came onto the bridge."

"We're almost to the end of it."

"Do they have vampire bats here?"

"I don't know. Probably." An instant later he added, "It seems they've discovered that just being in the same room with *any* bat can give you rabies."

They had come to high vegetation now. It was the end of the boardwalk. "I don't think I've ever seen so many fireflies," he mused.

"Rabies? That was in *Time*," she said accusingly. "I saw it."

"Therefore it's false. Is that it?"

Their heels no longer rapped in the silence; they were walking again on sand. Some of the houses here had thatched roofs. The banana leaves looked very green under the street lights. Not a person was visible.

"I'm being eaten by mosquitoes," she announced.

"Why don't we go back?"

"They're not going to stop just because we're walking the other way."

"The street lights end up ahead here," he said, pointing.

"All right." She swung sharply around and they began to walk in the other direction.

On the boardwalk, amid the clamor of the frogs, she told him, "I've got the horrors now. I'm going to hold my breath when I go under those bat trees."

"The mosquitoes are getting my ankles," he said. "I don't know why we came out this way."

She laughed her little-girl laugh. "I didn't choose it," she said gaily.

Once back on the ground, they got quickly to the plaza. There was one electric bulb burning on the hotel veranda. They went into the dark front hall, were met by the odor of garbage and cooking. Something moved at his side; Dr. Slade jumped and clicked on the flashlight. It was Mrs. Rainmantle sitting in a rocking chair in the dark.

"Oh, I've been waiting for you!" she cried, her voice calamitous. "I can't find anyone. They've *got* to give me a different room."

"Is it awful?" asked Mrs. Slade.

"There's no key in the door, no bolt, no possible way of locking it. I refuse to sleep in it, that's all." Her voice had risen; it was as if she were already making her official complaint.

Dr. Slade turned the flashlight's beam into distant corners. "Isn't there anybody around down here? Must be a watchman or somebody."

"Nobody! And there's the front door wide open. Anyway, the bed sags like a hammock. How are your beds?" There was the odor of fresh whiskey on her breath.

"They're all right," said Mrs. Slade.

"She's used to roughing it," explained her husband quickly.

"It's the door that makes the room impossible," Mrs. Rainmantle said in a dead voice. They were silent.

"Well, we might as well go up," Mrs. Slade said at last. "There's at least a light upstairs."

When they stood outside the Slades' bedroom Mrs. Rainmantle pushed on, crying, "Come in here. I want to show you." She led the way into the dark further chamber and turned on the light. The place was clearly nothing more than a storeroom for old pieces of furniture, with a crooked bed pushed into one corner. A ten-year-old calendar dangled by one corner on the wall beside the bureau. The air was hot and still.

"This is awful!" exclaimed Mrs. Slade. "I don't understand how they dare put anyone in a room like this."

A narrow passageway between the stacked chairs and Mrs. Rainmantle's unpacked valises made it just possible to get through to the bed.

"But look at the door!" cried Mrs. Rainmantle; her voice again sounded hysterical. "I'll sit downstairs out on the porch. Anywhere. It doesn't matter. I won't sleep here."

"Come into our room," Mrs. Slade urged her. "We can sit down."

At the far end of the veranda the light spilled out onto the boards through an open door. There was the faint sound of men's voices. Perhaps only two men, Dr. Slade thought, pausing to listen as he followed the two women from one room to the other; he got the impression that they were sitting over a bottle. He saw his wife lay her hand on the older woman's arm as they went through the door, and he had an immediate premonition of the way in which the situation was going to be resolved. Indeed, the ladies had scarcely sat down facing one another in the two chairs under the light before Mrs. Slade was saying, "You simply stay in here with me, Mrs. Rainmantle, and everything will be all right. Just forget about it."

"Oh, I couldn't!"

"Dr. Slade doesn't mind whether his door is locked or not. Do you, Taylor?"

"No, I don't mind," he said slowly.

"It doesn't matter to him, really," pleaded Mrs. Slade. "And it matters so much to you."

"Well," Mrs. Rainmantle sighed, looking at him timidly. "It *would* be a godsend."

"It's quite all right," he assured her. "Only I suggest we do it now." He wanted to be by himself quickly, so that his ill-humor should not become visible. But instead of leaving the room, he strode over to the wash basin and began to brush his teeth. "Excuse me if I do this," he said thickly, spitting into the basin. "I don't want to carry anything into the other room. Do you need anything of yours from there, Mrs. Rainmantle?"

She emerged from a brief reverie. "No, no. I have everything I want in my handbag."

"I'll pound on the door at half past five," he said to his wife. She was looking at him sadly, as if she suspected that there would be no swift forgiving of her treason. He stared at her with what he hoped was no expression at all and said, "Good night." "Good night," he said also to Mrs. Rainmantle, and then he was out of the room, having failed to take along any pajamas.

He'll sleep naked, she thought. She heard the door of the next room shut. The men down at the end of the balcony were still talking; the louder words made their sounds heard even above the insects.

Mrs. Rainmantle fished in her handbag and pulled out a pint of whiskey she had bought that afternoon at a Chinese shop on the waterfront. It was about half empty. "I'm going to have myself a little drink before I undress," she said with satisfaction, walking over to the washbasin. "One for you?"

"A nightcap."

33

She poured far too much Scotch into Mrs. Slade's glass, but being able to relax for a moment seemed to be giving her so much pleasure that Mrs. Slade did not protest.

"This may look like rank self-indulgence to you," began Mrs. Rainmantle, settling back in her chair, "but today was a day I'll always remember. And not for its pleasantness, either. *Nothing* happened the way it was supposed to."

Mrs. Slade thought: Does it ever?

"You must be very tired," she said, certain that the other expected a more lively demonstration of sympathy than she was giving her. She hoped that when she had drunk the whiskey she might feel more like going out of her way to say kind words. She looked at the wall and imagined her husband on the other side of it, unable to sleep in the leaning bed, trying to get into a bearable position, cursing the stagnant air and the smell of dust.

Mrs. Rainmantle was talking; it was a monologue and there seemed no need to listen carefully. She tried nevertheless to follow, fearing that otherwise her eyes would shut of their own accord.

"I want my house to have space in it," Mrs. Rainmantle declared. "I want my rooms to be enormous."

Although Mrs. Slade had drunk all the whiskey in her glass, the awaited feeling of benevolence toward her guest still had not manifested itself; she only wanted very much to go to bed.

She heard herself asking blankly, "Where is this house?"

"Oh, it's going to be in Hawaii. I've bought the property." Mrs. Rainmantle poured herself another small drink.

"How wonderful!" said Mrs. Slade.

"I really think I'm going to be happy there. In the end, living in hotel rooms is dehumanizing."

Some minutes later Mrs. Slade sprang up. "I've got to go to bed. I'm sorry."

"Yes, we must."

Through the confused folds of her mosquito netting she saw Mrs. Rainmantle go to the wall by the door and turn off the light. "Can you see to undress?" she asked.

"I never have any trouble undressing," Mrs. Rainmantle replied cheerfully from inside her garments.

She heard the other bed creak as it was charged with the weight of the heavy body. Mrs. Rainmantle sighed deeply. "It feels good," she said with contentment.

The insects sang, a door closed somewhere. Mrs. Slade wished she had refused the whiskey; it was the wrong thing to have put into her stomach. She tried hard not to think of Dr. Slade, lying in the awful room, but the image was there in front of her.

8

DR. SLADE SHUT HIS DOOR, undressed, and laid his clothes out along the top of the dusty bureau. When he was naked, he stood under the light and adjusted the alarm of his watch. Then, looking once apprehensively at the deformed bed, he switched off the light. With his flashlight he found his way through the chaos to the foot of the mosquito net and climbed up onto the bed. After a certain number of experiments he discovered that if he lay diagonally across its sloping surface he could be reasonably comfortable. Coming in here without pajamas had been purposeful on his part. It was a mute protest, a way of refusing the room existence. When morning came, he would dress and walk out of it empty-handed, as if he had never been aware of it. Underneath the encompassing sound of the insects he sometimes could hear the two women's voices, but not their words.

The smell of the dust was in the air inside here; his hot breath came back at him from the netting near his face. Mrs. Rainmantle, he thought wryly, had merely shown normal animal intelligence in refusing to use the room, lock or no lock on the door.

It had been his hope to sleep in the same bed with his wife, at least for a part of the night. The past two nights they had been on the ship, where the size and disposition of the berths had discouraged any project of lovemaking. The fantasy occurred to him that he might be doing a reckless thing in leaving Day alone with Mrs. Rainmantle; there was no certainty that she was not psychopathic. He tried to listen to the voices, to guess at the kind of conversation they were having, but he was getting sleepy, and the steady song of the night creatures filled the air. Surprised that it had been so easy, he recognized the fact that he was sliding down the incline into sleep.

His first thought when he heard the frantic buzzing of the alarm on his watch was that he had set it wrong; he had been ready to sleep, and he still had not achieved it. But when he pulled the flashlight out from under the pillow and turned it on, he saw that the time was five twenty-five. The sounds outside were entirely different now; the background consisted largely of isolated honks and chirps. Nearby a night bird of some sort made a series of clear low-pitched calls. Then he heard a second bird farther away, echoing the sound. He waited an instant and then, the flashlight still in his hand, he sprang out of bed and snapped the light switch. The room remained dark.

Soon he had his clothes on and was out on the veranda, rapping on the other door. He heard Day's muffled response and said quietly, "Five thirty."

"Yes," she answered. "Right."

There was no sign of dawn in the sky. The air was tepid and still. He went back into the dark room and, leaving the flashlight on, washed his face over the basin and combed his hair. He intended to shave the last thing before they left for the station.

He turned the flashlight off and sat down on the bed in the dark. Now the roosters were crowing in the distance, and dogs were barking, and below in the garden a cockatoo began to scream—probably the same bird they had heard at lunch the day before. The wandering fingers of a fresh predawn breeze reached him from time to time, and he thought, This is the good hour, when the stars are still shining and it's finally cool, and you can't see anything of the town.

He heard the key turn and the door of the next room open. Then there was the tapping of Mrs. Slade's mules along the veranda as she went in the direction of the bathrooms. The feeblest suggestion of daylight had begun to show in the sky; each minute it would be stronger. After a long time he heard the mules coming back, and then the door was shut again.

Mrs. Slade's night had been long and bristling with nightmares. She had lain on the sheet sweating inside the mosquito net, hating the room, hating even the idea

37

of poor Mrs. Rainmantle lying in all her flesh on the other bed. With the whiskey's acid flame still flickering in her stomach, she had forced herself to breathe slowly, regularly, but the possibility of being seized and paralyzed by her own nightmare and never been far off. How many times had she forced herself to turn over in the bed to dispel the forming tornado of dreams? At first, during her waking spells, she had listened intently in order to pick out, this side of the screaming metallic backdrop, the nearer, softer sound of Mrs. Rainmantle's snoring. Sometimes, aware of the open window, she was certain that a third presence had come into the room. She would fix a point in the dark, her eyes very wide, and lie absolutely still, trying to breathe like someone asleep. Once she had felt a heavy insect or a lizard land on the canopy above her head, and remain clinging there, moving the netting lightly from time to time. Then there had been only the monstrous hairy darkness that clicked and pulsed out there from its black insect throat.

She had not dared, even with her flashlight, to get out of bed to look for a Seconal, for fear of stepping on a scorpion or a centipede, and so she had lain there in a suspended state between sleeping and waking. When the knock came at the door, she said, "Uh," and, seizing the flashlight as if it had been a weapon, tore open the netting and stood upright on the floor to play the beam around the room. In the dimness she could distinguish Mrs. Rainmantle's body like a great pillow entangled with the sheets on the far side of the bed. She moved the beam along the wall. There by the door was the light switch. She walked over and pushed it. The light did not come on. It was still night—the same night; her stomach burned and her head ached. Dr. Slade was knocking on the door. Suddenly she was fearful that Mrs. Rainmantle would waken. She put her face near the panel of the door and said calmly, "Yes. Right." It stopped the knocking, and she heard him go back into his room.

A moment later she hurried out toward the bathroom, cursing the plants as they rubbed against her face in the dark. Even before she got to the end of the balcony she realized that she was not going to take a shower. There would be nowhere to put the flashlight; it would get wet or fall off onto the floor, and she would be there in the dark with the water running over her. She went into one of the rooms and locked the door behind her. It was hot, dark, airless. A small table stood between the washbasin and the shower. She set the flashlight down. The walls were impregnated with the ancient stench of the latrine. Later, when the sun was up, she would be all right, she knew, but at the moment she felt ill. If I can throw it up, she thought. But it was as impossible as trying to retch up the night; the night was still there, and the fiery sourness still inside her.

When she came out, the air seemed a little cooler, and she could almost see her way through the ferns and palms without the flashlight. She pressed it intermittently as she walked along; when she got to her room she turned it all the way on, went in, and shut the door. In order to minimize the chances of waking Mrs. Rainmantle (for she did not relish the idea of having to talk with her at this point) she got into her clothing quickly and silently. Then she packed her two cases and gathered up her handbag, all the while reflecting that it was going to seem a little unfriendly of her to run off this way without saying goodbye. No. We've got to go, she told herself; she wanted to get out of the room once and for all. The surest way for her to accomplish this was for her to pack Taylor's things herself and set all the lug-

39

gage outside the door. That way the room would remain quiet. He would not have to come in at all, and Mrs. Rainmantle would go on sleeping.

She had his bags shut in a minute; he had taken practically nothing out of them. She opened the door onto the veranda. Slowly, one by one, she carried the suitcases out and set them down, making as little sound as possible. Then, when everything was out, she stood in the doorway and played the flashlight rapidly once around the room, saying a silent goodbye to Mrs. Rainmantle as it reached her corner. The beam went on along the wall past the mirror and coat hooks.

She shut the door and stood perfectly still, listening for a sound from within, and trying to be certain of what she had just seen. Mrs. Rainmantle still lay in her uncomfortable position on the wall side of the bed, and one great leg hung over the edge. In that instant of faint light, and with the draperies of the mosquito netting in the way, she could not be certain, but it seemed to her that Mrs. Rainmantle's eyes had been open. Her reaction had been to pull the door shut even more quickly. And now she listened. If Mrs. Rainmantle were awake, it was likely that even at this moment she was getting up and coming to the door.

There was no sound from inside the room. She tried to recapture the picture once more as she had seen it. The eyes seemed to be shut this time. But then it became like a chromolithograph of Jesus where the closed lids suddenly flew open and the eyes were there, looking straight ahead. She turned and knocked on Dr. Slade's door.

9

Following the course of a roaring stream, the small train wound slowly uphill. Tree smells and birdsong blew in through the open windows. At the hotel they had managed to get only coffee; breakfast had been some bananas bought through the car window before the train had pulled out of Puerto Farol. One sickly boy had been available to carry the luggage to the station, instead of the three men Dr. Slade had asked for. They had made the train only by dividing the valises among them, with Mrs. Slade carrying a basket and her own overnight bag.

Her headache, largely dissipated by the coffee, had revived during the rush to the station. Now, as the train swerved violently from one side to the other, an occasional throb made her wince. She took a pair of dark glasses from her handbag and put them on. A moment later she slipped her hand into the bag again and began to touch the objects there, until she had found a tube of Optalidon, which she surreptitiously removed. While Dr. Slade was occupied in looking at the landscape she popped one of the pills into her mouth, but apparently he had noticed the motion of her hand, out of the corner of his eye. He turned to look at her.

"You sleep all right?"

"Did *you?*" she countered. The night was too recent for her to want to discuss it. "You had a horrible bed."

"I slept fine," he said, still looking at her. "I could have done with a little more, yes."

She wanted to change the subject, but she could not

think of anything to talk about. It was as though her mind were working there in her head all by itself, hoping to find an answer to an unformulated question.

Perhaps an hour and a half later they were atop the first ridge of sierra, overlooking the misty green coastal plain. The wind that came in through the windows was suddenly cold. Dr. Slade slipped on his jacket.

"Are you chilly?" he said.

"No."

She would have been happy to sit back and tell Taylor how strange Mrs. Rainmantle had looked, and how it had made her feel at the time, after she had shut the door. It would have been a relief to describe how she had kept thinking of it since. But if she began to talk about it, she would see again the circle of dim yellow light moving along the discolored wall, and Mrs. Rainmantle's head lying at an unlikely angle to the mountainous body, with the sheet pulled tight around her neck. If she got that far, she knew she would find the eyes open, staring senselessly out through the netting. She put her hand quickly to her face to keep the picture from forming. Seeing that Dr. Slade was watching her, she pretended to have a cinder in her eye. If he suspected any preoccupation in her, he would end by prying it all out; it was his belief that what he called negative emotions immediately ceased to exist once they had been exposed to the blazing light of reason. He would force her to put it into words, and words in this case were not what she wanted: they might only make it all the more real.

There was a forty-minute stop at a place called Tolosa, a pockmarked, dusty town with a short main street that ran along beside the railroad track. In company with a few passengers from the train they walked to a shabby restaurant opposite the station. The two elderly Chinese men who ran the place clearly had no interest in food.

"Nothing Chinese at all?" said Dr. Slade wistfully to the one who stood before them. The man said something in unintelligible Spanish and brought them the same dishes they had eaten back in Puerto Farol: brown beans, rice, plantain and fried eggs.

"This would have been a shock to Ruth," murmured Dr. Slade. "You know, the Chinese were the only good cooks in the world. But this is unbelievable. These two don't eat this food. They have their own in the kitchen."

Ruth had been Dr. Slade's first wife. By tacit mutual consent they never spoke of her. He supposed the understanding between them was a product of atavism: by itself it had come into being. Mention of the first Mrs. Slade was thus uncommon enough to make Day now look up from her plate. Then she understood that he had been expecting exactly that reaction, had provoked it purposely in order to be able to catch her eye and smile encouragingly at her. He's doing his best, she thought, resentful of having failed to conceal her nervousness. As if there had been no maneuver on his part, she smiled blandly. "The rice grains are fairly separate, at least," she said, looking back down at her plate. "I don't really mind this sort of bad food. There's so little difference here between good and bad, it doesn't matter much one way or the other."

She stopped talking and stared for a moment out into the bright sunlight. The train was there in front of her, stretching to left and right of the station. Everyone was leaning out of the car windows, buying food and soft drinks. Beyond was the open countryside of distant barren mountains and nearby wasteland. A factory siren wailed. She went on eating; Dr. Slade said nothing.

Back in their compartment, however, they both felt better. It was a relief to be on the train rather than looking across at it, expecting to see it start up without them. They relaxed and slept a while.

When Mrs. Slade awoke her headache was gone; she remained lying stretched out on the seat. Just after sunset, when they were scarcely an hour from the capital, the ticket collector came in, and she sat upright. The man went back out into the corridor and shut the door. Still they did not speak, their heads nodding with the movement of the train as they looked out at the red landscape and the coming of dusk across it. Some time after the rhythms of the train had taken over her consciousness although her eyes were still open, he said unexpectedly, "I wonder if she got in touch with her son today."

Mrs. Slade heard her own voice saying unsurely, "No . . ."

"You don't think she did?"

She shook her head with impatience. "I don't know any more than you do about it. I was thinking of something else."

10

AFTER MIDNIGHT THE CAPITAL was deserted; the long straight avenues, sparsely illumined, stretched for great distances into the stony plain beyond. For an hour or two the cold mountain wind swept over the highland, and after that the air was still. There were long periods during the night when the silence was like a fine needle in her ears. But a locomotive sometimes whistled from far out in the country as the train labored up a barranca from a lower valley. Or a caged bird in someone's patio nearby called a few clear notes. A cricket chirped, a plane flew overhead, far above even the invisible mountain peaks, and the *guardia* blew his soft pipe in the street below; in the lower part of the city the cathedral clock chimed the hour. With the silences in between, the night passed.

At the desk she had asked for a separate room. "What I really need is sleep," she told Dr. Slade. "I didn't sleep last night." Knowing she had already told him this, she was about to elaborate.

Dr. Slade spoke first. "Of course. Naturally."

When the bellboys let them into the room meant for her, she walked ahead of them to the window, opened it, and looked down at the tops of the trees in the dark street below. She listened.

"It's sublimely quiet."

She lay on the bed, comfortable in the cold dry air that came in through the window. Even now she did not feel sleepy; she supposed it was due to the altitude. It was a joy merely to lie still and be comfortable. The quiet room and the soft bed relaxed her; there were the added luxuries of feeling secure and being alone. A little before dawn she slept.

Dr. Slade woke and telephoned downstairs for breakfast. In the bathroom he dashed cold water into his eyes, seized a bath towel, and, after vigorously drying himself, stepped onto the small balcony outside his window. The city shone in the strong early sunlight, and the tops of the mountains looked absurdly near. His eye moved down the slopes to the forested regions, the lesser summits, and the vast detailed countryside of hills and valleys still lower down.

On his breakfast tray was a newspaper bearing a gummed label: BUENOS DÍAS. LA DIRECCIÓN. GOOD MORNING. THE MANAGEMENT. The coffee was good, and there was a big pitcher of it. He glanced at the headlines and poured himself another cup. Presently he got up, shaved, dressed, and went downstairs to look for a barbershop. There was none in the hotel; the desk clerk suggested he take a cab to the center of the city.

He decided to walk. It would be downhill nearly all the way. The shabby provincial capital was saved from ugliness only by its trees and parks. When he was seated in the swivel chair and covered by the sheet, the barber handed him a newspaper, which, even as he accepted it, he recognized as the same one that had been sent upstairs with his breakfast. He ran his eye over *El Globo*'s already familiar front page; a short item at the bottom caught his attention. The dateline contained the words *Puerto Farol*. He read on, his mouth dropping open. It was the account of a fire, which shortly after daybreak the preceding morning had destroyed a part of the Gran Hotel de la Independencia. It had claimed the life of one guest, Mrs. Agnes Rainmantle, a tourist of Canadian nationality who had arrived on the M.S. *Cordillera*. There was a description of the property damage caused to the building, and that was all, save that the piece ended with the words *"a lamentar,"* which somehow removed it from the realm of the serious or possible. No further disgraces to lament!

Poor woman, he thought, his natural chagrin weighted

by a small sense of guilt because he had been rude to her at the end of her last evening.

Day mustn't see this, he said to himself suddenly. I've got to keep it away from her.

11

MRS. SLADE OPENED HER EYES and looked at her watch: five minutes past eleven. Six hours, more or less, she thought; it was not really enough sleep, but she felt wide-awake and full of energy. She called down for breakfast and took a quick shower. When the maid arrived she had her set the tray on the balcony, and there in the hot sunlight she drank her coffee and ate her toast. There was a local newspaper on the tray; without looking at it she laid it on the table. Only when she had finished breakfast did she call Dr. Slade's room. There was no answer. He's rushed out to see the town, she thought, feeling a faint resentment that he should have gone without her, yet aware that had he come to her room and wakened her she would have been furious. She dressed and decided to take a short walk herself, while the morning smell was still in the air. Yesterday's nervousness was gone.

It was cool enough at last to wear the new pink linen suit she had been longing to put on. Its color complemented her suntan in a manner she had only partially foreseen. From the closet mirror she walked out onto the terrace and lit a cigarette while she stood looking down across the red tile roofs of the city. The towering distant mountains behind it looked nearer than the town itself, half lost down there in its pool of haze. She tapped her ashes into the street, put on her sunglasses, and went back into the bedroom.

In the lobby, next to the reception desk, there was a small brightly lighted newsstand, and in front of it an assortment of comfortable chairs, each with its reading lamp. At the moment the reception hall was empty of guests save for one young man, who was sprawled in one of the chairs, his legs over the side, reading a magazine.

At the counter she examined the display of newspapers from two and three days earlier, choosing a San Francisco *Chronicle* and a New York *Times*. A man appeared from an inner room and stood facing her; she asked him for *Newsweek* and handed him a banknote. "Oh," he said, looking at it. "Excuse me one minute." He went back into the room where he had been.

Wheeling slowly around, she leaned against the counter, her hands behind her, and gazed across the lobby. It surprised her to see it so empty at this hour of the morning. Although she told herself that she did not particularly want to, she glanced again at the young man and found herself forming an opinion. If a man was wholly and dramatically handsome, she looked for a character defect. To her way of thinking, no man could look as this one did and not have ended by taking unfair advantage of it.

The young man flicked his cigarette ashes into a tall jar by his hand, and went on reading. She turned back to the stand; the man counted out her change for her. "Did you take out for *Newsweek*?" she asked him, run-

48

ning her eye over the display of publications. "Where is it?"

"*Newsweek?* You come back in one-half hour."

There was a small garden off the lobby, crowded with philodendron and cages of parakeets. She chose a comfortable chair in the sun, put on her dark glasses, and sat there reading the newspapers for exactly thirty minutes, expecting Dr. Slade to appear at any moment. Then, convinced that the clerk behind the desk would not yet have managed to get hold of her magazine, and not much caring, she went back to ask him.

The young man, still in his armchair, took no notice of her as she went past. Even as she approached the counter and saw the face of the clerk behind it, she knew she had been right. "No more *Newsweek!*" he cried in an unnecessarily loud voice. "All sold out."

There was a movement behind her; she turned and saw the young man advancing. He held several magazines out in front of him and smiled tentatively. "I'm sorry," he told her. "I couldn't help hearing. Here's a *Newsweek.* I've got one here. Will you take it?"

The tone of her voice as she said, "No. No, thank you," made her feel that she was being unfriendly, and so she smiled back and added, "I wouldn't have read it anyway. You keep it."

He still held it out. "I've looked at it. You won't find another anywhere else in town. They all go the first few hours."

She had no intention of accepting the magazine. "It's not important," she said. "It doesn't matter at all. They don't sell books anywhere here in the hotel, do they?"

The man behind the counter had disappeared into the inner room, and the young man was holding a pack of

49

cigarettes in front of her. She took one. As he lighted it
for her he was saying, "There's only one store in town
where you can get books in English. I've got my car
outside."

She was tempted, but she hesitated. "Oh," she said.
"You see, I'm sort of expecting to see my husband here
in the lobby any minute." It seemed an ungracious way
of refusing, and it was not what she had meant to say.

The young man stepped over to the reception desk
and spoke briefly with the clerk. She stood there with
the cigarette in her hand, thankful now that there was
no one else to witness the equivocal scene. He came
back, smiling more broadly. "Your husband's gone to the
barbershop," he told her. "So it's up to you."

The long open convertible had a crumpled fender.

"You *are* American?" she said. The motor roared and
they moved ahead through the shadows of the high
trees.

He laughed. "No! I'm just another irresponsible citizen.
I've lived here so long I'm one of them."

That's no answer, she thought, nettled.

The streets in the lower city were narrow and crowded
with traffic. "I'm enjoying this," she told him. Again he
made an ambiguous reply. "Why not?" he said brightly.

She chose three paperbacks in swift succession while
he watched. "Something to look at in bed," she said over
her shoulder while she paid the woman.

"Good to have," he answered, and she turned further
and glanced at him. His smile was there, but it said
nothing.

"I'm glad to know about this place," she went on. "I'll
come down again when I can look around."

"Take as long as you like."

She laughed and stepped ahead of him through the

doorway. "I've got plenty for now," she told him. "I'm really delighted."

The car moved up a long steep ramp lined with palms and azaleas. At the top there was a park with a railing that ran along the edge of a cliff, where crowds of people leaned, looking down at the city in the haze below.

"You understand I've got to go to the hotel," she began, trying to make the words sound like a command and immediately aware of her failure.

"Look up there!" the young man said. He pointed to the summit of a steep green slope where a few dozen high pines grew; a large white building towered above them.

"I'm going to be a bore now," she warned him. "Is this the way to the hotel?"

"It's one way," he replied, turning toward her and shaking his head sadly. "You imagining what it would be like to be kidnaped? Snatched by somebody who hasn't got money on his mind at all, never gets in touch with anybody, just keeps you there, on and on? Now, *that* would be something to worry about."

"I'll worry about it when I come to it," she said crisply. "You mean you're taking a long way around; isn't that it?"

He looked at her again, this time with amazement. "You're a nervous one, aren't you? We've been gone about twenty minutes so far. We'll be back at the hotel in another twenty. How's that?"

"It's not tragic, I suppose. You did say ten originally, if you remember."

He finally spoke, after he had navigated the last hairpin curve. "Twenty minutes. Eighteen now. I give you my word."

They came out on top of the hill. The tall white building was an apartment house, and he stopped the car in front of it. Then he got out and came around to her door. "Come up for a minute. I want to get a jacket."

"What about the seventeen minutes?"

"That's only if you don't argue." He opened the door. She picked up her handbag and the parcel and got out. As they went into the building she had an impression of glass and metal, rocks and plants. In the elevator mirror she saw that her hair had been blown into an unrecognizable shape. "The wind has ruined me," she complained, fussing with it.

"You can fix it upstairs," he told her.

They went to the top. The door opened onto a patio where a jet of water splashed into a pool. There was a colonnade on the right, a short flight of steps to go down, and they walked into a vast room.

"It's breathtaking," she said; at the same time, her opinion of him dropped still further. She went slowly down the steps. "I'd hate to be responsible for keeping this place clean." She wanted him to know that she thought it impractical, absurd, for a young man to have such an excessively luxurious apartment.

She sat down. "It's all leather, fur and glass!" she exclaimed.

"There's no problem," he told her, looking mildly surprised. "The air's free of dust up here. What can I give you? Want to fix your hair? In there, through that door, and I'll make you a drink. A quick vodka martini?"

She gave a deliberately mirthless laugh. "Go on. I can't stop you."

The wall in front of her was entirely hidden by a barrage of trees and vines that reached to the ceiling; illumined dimly from within, it gave her the feeling of being at the edge of a forest. Sweet-smelling mountain air moved slowly through the room, stirring the upper tendrils and fronds. Somewhere out in the bright daylight a military band was playing; the distant sounds floated up on the breeze, now louder, now softer. She ran her hand tentatively over the vicuña skin that covered the couch where she sat. Then she rose and went to arrange her hair in the little room he had indicated.

From some part of the apartment she heard the clear voice of a small child call out, "Where, Mommy?" Standing before the mirror, drawing her upper lip taut over her teeth as she applied her lipstick, she realized with faint astonishment that she had not foreseen a wife. Why not? she wondered.

There were sounds in the big room. "Your drink's here," he called.

"Well, that was quick!" She came out of the dressing room to join him.

He had his glass in his hand, was in fact already drinking from it. She lifted hers from the tray; it was very cold. "Come on outside," he told her.

On the terrace there was a grotto with a pool inside it, and a stream that ran in a crooked course, winding among the groups of chairs and tables. Below was the city with its far-off murmur, and on all sides the sky was cut across by the mountains' gray crests. "This is magnificent!" she exclaimed when they got to the edge and looked out.

He drained his glass. "When you've got the scenery in front of you, you take advantage of it, no?"

"You have a child here," she said; it was not a question, but its inflection demanded a reply. "I heard it talking."

"In this country you never know whether it's a child or a parrot," he told her, looking very serious.

"What *I* heard sounded very much like a child." She was not used to being put off in this manner.

"It probably was a child, then. There's one here. It's time to go. Seven minutes."

Before they got to the door, she took a last look around the terrace. "It gives me such a wonderful feeling of *freedom*," she said, and stepped inside.

They drove through a short stretch of forest, and down the side of the mountain to a boulevard that led to the hotel. This time she kept her hands over her hair. He drew up at the entrance and stopped the car.

"Have I been exact?" He looked at his wristwatch.

"Yes, indeed, you've been exact," she said, delighted with the episode, now that she was back and it was over. "And you've been very kind."

They got out and stood on the sidewalk in the sun. "How about tomorrow?" he said suddenly. "You and your husband. You and Dr. Slade. I'd like to have you meet Luchita."

"Oh," she said. "Yes. Well, when I've met *you*, maybe you can arrange it."

"The name's Soto." She had the impression that it was an unpleasant experience for him to have to pronounce it; at the same time he drew himself up and looked at her defiantly. "S—O—T—O. Easy. If we make it around six-thirty you'll get the sunset. Try and persuade the doctor. I'll pick you up right here. Why don't I phone you around ten tomorrow morning?"

"I think ten would be fine," she said.

He got into the car, backed, smiling at her, eased ahead, waved slowly once, and drove off. She heard him opening the motor up as the car sped down the boulevard.

On her way across the lobby the clerk at the newsstand called out to her, "That's a very fine young man, Mr. Soto!"

She glanced with apprehension around the lobby: it was as empty as it had been before. At least, she thought, if she went nearer to the counter he would lower his voice. "Yes?" she said, walking over to within a few paces of him.

"Ah, yes! A very important family. His father is Don José García Soto. But he don't like *him*." He smiled and shrugged; apparently that was the end of the story, even though the emphasis on the final "him" made its meaning ambiguous.

"His father doesn't like him, you mean?"

"No. He don't like *him*."

Since the words had been said in precisely the same way as before, she did not know whether to understand it as a correction or a reiteration. "Why not?" she asked him, thinking she might get at it that way.

He wagged his head from side to side. "Young man, he likes a good time. The old man, he don't go with that, he don't see it the same way. So what they going to do?"

Dr. Slade had taken a cab back to the hotel. In a quiet corner of the lounge, behind a screen of climbing plants, he caught sight of Mrs. Slade standing by a counter, engaged in conversation with the clerk. Always he made a point of leaving her the maximum of privacy and freedom of movement. And now, although he thought of joining her, he decided not to, and continued through the lobby to the elevators. As he stood waiting, a *botónes*

55

in a brilliant green uniform came running up to him, crying, "*Señor!*"

He followed the boy back to the newsstand. While he bent to kiss her, she said with an admonitory smile, "I saw you sneak by."

They walked slowly through the lobby.

"Better today?"

"Yes. I'm fine. I had a ride."

"Who with? Where to?"

She sighed. It seemed suddenly tedious to have to tell the story. "Somebody. I don't know. His name is Soto."

"Well, well!" He smiled at her, and as always she was aware of the beam of ownership in his eyes. "Why don't we eat? Do you want to go up to your room first?"

"No."

"I'm going up for a minute," he told her. "I'll be right down."

His bedroom had been made up; there was a bowl of wine-colored dahlias on the coffee table. He noted with approval that the window had been left open and the curtains drawn. *El Globo* lay on the desk. He folded and refolded it, until he had made it as small as possible. Then he took it out onto the balcony and dropped it over the railing. He watched it hit the paving stones below. The leaves of the trees down there glistened in the mid-day sunlight.

At lunchtime the hotel's dining room was crowded with the sleek upper-class local population. "Here where they don't need it they've got air conditioning," Dr. Slade remarked. Because he felt well, he was still delighted with the climate. "It's like a spring day out."

"Ideal," she agreed. "He had an open car, and I'm already dead. I got to sleep sometime this morning."

"Not again!" he said, frowning.

56

"No," she corrected him. "I *slept,* at least. Night before last I didn't sleep."

"You may have dropped off even then," he said in a matter-of-fact tone. "It often happens during those bad nights. Only you don't remember it."

Not listening, she went back to eating her melon.

"Who's this who took you in his car?"

She ran through the principal points in the encounter. "He's invited us out for drinks with them tomorrow night."

Dr. Slade frowned again. She knew him well enough to be certain he was thinking that people ought to be thoroughly scrutinized before one accepted invitations from them. "Well," he said, "if you've just been there, I should think it would be better to have them here, wouldn't it?"

Up until then she had felt indifferent to the invitation. Now that he seemed on the point of refusing it, she found that on the contrary she was rather eager to go. "They have a spectacular apartment. I just got a glimpse of it for a minute. We stopped on the way up from the bookstore. I didn't even see *her.*"

When lunch was over, they went upstairs. She slept immediately. At four o'clock she was up, tapping on his door.

"Let's go out for a walk this minute while the sun's still shining," she said, peering into his room from the corridor.

The hotel was not far from the edge of town. From a pavilion in a park higher up they watched the sun set behind the mountains and the valley come alive with the lights of the capital.

"The city looks so small, doesn't it, in the middle of all these mountains," she said with wonder.

"There's supposed to be a pretty good nightclub, called the Costa de Oro," he told her. They never went out at night without having a lengthy discussion afterwards whose point was to prove that the excursion had been an indefensible waste of time and money.

"It might be fun some night," she said uncertainly. Then she added in a hearty voice, "Tonight I'm going to sleep or know the reason why."

"Of course, you've got to sleep," he said gravely.

The early night wind, spiced with the smell of pine, had begun to stir through the valley. They shivered and started to walk briskly down the hill; on the way out of the park they found a taxi.

TWO

12

WHAT HAD HAPPENED WAS that Luchita, unusually ingenuous for her seventeen years, had made a serious miscalculation. To her it had seemed reasonable, and therefore likely, that if Vero were willing to supply fifty dollars a week and allow Pepito and her to live with him, Señor Guzman, who was middle-aged and much more difficult in his demands, would at least furnish her fare back to Paris. Thus, observing what she imagined was the greatest secrecy, she had "escaped" from Vero and gone to live with Señor Guzman. (Even now, when she had been back at Vero's for three weeks, she did not know that Vero and Señor Guzman had discussed the switch in detail before the idea of making it had occurred to her.) All she had to show for her trouble was three pairs of shoes, a wristwatch, and a transistor tape recorder covered in lizard skin; and although Señor Guzman had pointed out to her that the aggregate value of these items was a good deal more than the seventy-five dollars a week he had vaguely mentioned at the outset, she had decided after a fortnight to return to Vero.

He took her back into the household with good grace, but in the meantime he had made some new laws. Pepito was to sleep in one of the servants' rooms and at no time was to be allowed beyond the kitchen, while she, instead of occupying the big blue room with her favorite bathroom, was to share Vero's room with him. She had objected strongly to this last provision; not that she minded the loss of privacy, but the arrangement clearly lowered her bargaining power. However, the situation at

Señor Guzman's had been growing steadily more unbearable; twice he had found her *yerba* and thrown it out, so that she had had to spend a lot of time and money getting more, and when Pepito had tossed his iron locomotive and broken the big mirror in the dining room, Señor Guzman had hit him in the face with the back of his hand, so hard that the big diamond ring had cut his cheek. While she was crying in her room afterwards, she had decided that there was something wrong with Señor Guzman and that it would be better for her to get out of his house.

The day she had gone back to see Vero she had done without smoking for hours beforehand, trying to plan the course of the conversation they would have, at the same time certain that however it went, it would be completely different from the way she was imagining it. This proved to be the case. He merely nodded his head now and then while she was talking, and suddenly expounded the new laws which would apply if she returned. Then he held his cigarette case in front of her, snapped it open, and said, "The filter tips." And she pulled out a fat grifa and lit it. Afterwards she thought it had been this gesture which had made her decide to accept the new laws and the change in her status they implied. It was impossible to live with a man who never smoked anything but tobacco, who hated even the smell of marijuana and could detect it in the air an hour afterward, and who thought he had the right to go through her bags in his search for hidden stores of it.

Before the "escape," the rule with Vero had been three times a week. She never knew which nights, because sometimes he liked them one after the other, and sometimes he spaced them. Now that she was going to sleep

62

in his room, she suspected that she would have no more free nights at all.

The evening of her return they were talking across the space between the two beds. "I want you to be civilized," he was telling her. "That means you should do exactly as you feel like doing. But you have to *know* you want to do it, and know *why* you want to, too."

"I know what I want," she said, blinking her eyes. "I want to go to Paris. But I'm not civilized, am I? Because I haven't got the money for the ticket. *La plata, hombre, la plata!*"

"I'm trying to explain something and you're wailing about Paris. Why don't we finish one thing first?"

"You want to finish something?" she demanded fiercely. "I want to finish something, too. I want to say goodbye to this lousy country. The people! The way they act! *Petits bourgeois!* Pah!" She raised herself and remained leaning on one elbow. "If it's true you want to see me be civilized, you know how to do it. Let me go to Paris. I don't care if it's on a ship, tourist class. If you want to see me lying dead, leave me here longer, that's all."

Luchita had learned English in her native Havana; Spanish she spoke here only with the servants, and occasionally when she had smoked heavily and was feeling exceptionally *cotorra*. This was not the case tonight; the effects of her morning grifas were dissipated, and with an eye to being as astute as possible in the argument she expected, she had not smoked since lunch.

"You won't listen! You won't let me talk!" he was complaining. Then he lowered his voice. "You know what I was really talking about? You *want* to know?"

"Yes," she said in a small voice, but guardedly.

63

"I was trying to say that whenever you want to go to the Embajadores or the Tahiti or any of those places, go ahead. If you really want to go and you know why, then go on. When you'd rather stay here and be with me, here I am!" He held out his arms as if in expectation of an embrace.

She smiled. "That's very sweet," she said, lying down, talking into the pillow. "You do trust me, Vero."

"Of course I do. I practically always have."

She sat up again. "Well, thank God!" she cried with feeling, and slowly let her head fall back onto the pillow.

"I don't trust all of *them*, I can tell you that," he went on. "Not when they buy a hundred dollars' worth of pictures all at once. Come on!" he said, angry suddenly that she should be making sounds of protest. "I saw him. I saw where his hand was. I don't have to listen to anything."

"Because you think the pictures stink," she said bitterly.

He was dramatically silent for a moment. "Have I ever said they stank?"

"But you can't believe somebody could like them."

"Not that much, no! There's a limit to everything."

"Well, thank God Mr. Mason's limit's not your limit. At least I'm a hundred dollars nearer to Paris."

"What is it? Can't you wait till June? Or don't you believe me, or what?"

"How do I know what to believe?" she demanded fiercely. "You say you'll have it. But you said that before and you didn't have it."

"I'll have it," he said quietly.

She lay on her stomach and kicked her feet up and down in the air. "Oh, if I could really be sure!" she cried. "You know I'd stay every night with you, and the hell with the pictures." She sat up once more and looked across at him. "But I can't be sure! I've got to keep going until I see the ticket in my hand."

"You're free, tan, and seventeen," he said. "You do just what you feel you ought to do."

"Wait." She slid down off the bed, put on a peignoir and went out to the kitchen. Pepito's room gave onto a narrow corridor beyond.

She opened the door; Pepito was sleeping. From the bookcase she took a small metal box and carried it back with her into the bedroom. The jazz was playing very softly behind the plants on the terrace. She got into his bed beside him and took a cigarette from the box. It was one of the last batch she had rolled, two days before, at Señor Guzman's.

"I'm sleepy," she told him. "I'm going to turn on a little. I can go to the Embajadores tomorrow."

Later, a little before daybreak, she murmured, "I do love you, Vero, and Pepito loves you too. Why won't you be sweet to us? Why?"

She had long been aware that these attempts at persuasion, ill-timed or not, were useless, but the image kept suggesting itself to her: she was letting herself into the apartment with her own keys because she was the *señora,* and Pepito was running in to meet her from the big terrace, where even at the beginning he had never been allowed to go.

"You know the whole goddamned story," he said yawning. "You wouldn't even have your fifty a week."

"Don José García Soto," she intoned scornfully. "The lousy *bourgeois!* Do I talk about my grandfather's uncle? He was the Cardinal Gonsalvez y Alcántara, and so what?"

"So he knows you're from a good family. Jesus!" He

was silent an instant before going on. "Can't you understand he doesn't give a shit *who* you are? He doesn't like you. It's simple."

"You don't have to use that talk with me."

She knew she was not going to be able to extend the argument into new territory, into regions that had not already been covered on other occasions, but the subject was always there, and it was irresistible. "Because I don't hang furs on me like the *putas* at his house."

"Yes! You've said it!" he cried. "A lot of it's the way you look. You had time to change the other night. You didn't have to come in to dinner with dirt on your face, and wearing those stinking Levis. You're just a lazy little slut."

She hit him with her fist on the shoulder as hard as she could, sprang out of bed, and stood there naked, looking down at him. "You take his side now," she whispered, as if the thought were more than she could bear. "I knew you were just like him."

"Agh!" he said with disgust, and rolled over to sleep.

Luchita got into her bed. Listening to the sounds of the waking city, she thought once again about Paris.

13

OTHER NIGHTS SINCE THEN had been much the same; she did go a few times to the nightclubs and even managed to sell several more pictures, although she told Vero it had been only two. It seemed logical to her that the less she appeared to be earning, the more generous he would be when the moment came to supply her with passage money to Paris. As the days went by, she found herself almost believing him when he assured her that the money was going to be available. There was no single reason for the change in the way she felt; it could have been a combination of several things. Vero had never talked with her very much in any case, but now he spoke practically not at all unless they were in bed. He would lie naked on the terrace all day, reading; then he would dress and go out with friends to dinner, and she would not see him until he came home to bed. Twice he had taken her out to a Chinese roadhouse at kilometer 12 on the highway. She had enjoyed the dancing after dinner, but the clientele was pitifully provincial; she told him so, and it put him into a bad humor.

During the most recent days, Vero had been seeing a good deal more of Thorny, whom she disliked increasingly. "I hate the way he smiles," she told Vero. "Thank God Pepito lives with the servants. At least he can't see Thorny." Then she added suspiciously, "What does he want?"

"Want? He doesn't want anything as far as I know. I'm taking him down to the ranch this weekend."

She looked at him unbelievingly. "Vero, you're crazy," she declared. "Why do you want to take him down there?"

"Because he's working for me. Is that important to you?"

Luchita was contemptuous. "Work? What sort of work could Thorny do? He's never worked in his life."

"Yes, yes, yes. I know," Vero said patiently. "For the

record, he did have a job once at Radio Nacional. But anyway, he's got one now for a few weeks. He's going to put in the sound system for me."

"Thorny?"

"He's going to supervise, for God's sake! Make them follow my instructions. If they're left alone there, they'll do it all ass backwards. What difference does it make to you whether Thorny's down at the ranch or not?"

"I don't like him," she said simply.

He laughed. "You're not going to be there."

"Me at San Felipe? I'd rather be in jail!"

He looked at her darkly. "You seemed to enjoy yourself all right."

She was evasive. "Snakes and centipedes, and the vines always slap you in the face. And so hot, my God!" She opened her mouth and gasped, remembering it.

"You never saw a snake the whole time you were there."

"I saw a centipede."

"It's an old house. They're in the foundation."

"In this country," she told him, "there's only one thing worse than the mountains, and that's your lousy *tierra caliente*."

Thorny came at eight on Friday morning. They took the station wagon because they were going to pick up farm implements and parts for a new generator on the way out of the city. As soon as Vero had left, Luchita went hunting through his bedroom and bathroom, collecting her things. She had decided to sleep on the couch in Pepito's room for the two nights, and she wanted to move her effects quickly, before Paloma, the housemaid, saw her and got her into conversation about her reasons. When she was alone she smoked more, out of nervousness. But the result of the smoking was to make her apprehensive; she knew she would sleep better locked into the little room with Pepito than by herself in the big bedroom where the masses of plants and the high screens frightened her.

When she had carried everything through the apartment to Pepito's room, she lay back on the couch against the cushions and lit a grifa. Pepito was kneeling on a chair opposite, playing with something on the table.

"Mommy, what's this?"

She looked up through the smoke and saw that he had found her handbag and was holding up some partially folded banknotes.

"What do you mean, what is it? It's money. Put it back."

"I know," he said, suddenly looking worldly-wise. "If we had money we'd go to Paris, wouldn't we?"

She stared at him in admiration; for a boy of five he was quick.

"You remember Paris: *Abuelita* and the bird in the cage?" she said hopefully.

"No."

"The green bird that used to say, '*Apaga la luz, hombre!*' And everybody used to laugh? You remember him."

"I do not!" Pepito said, looking intently at her.

"It was only a year ago." She fell silent, to think about Paris. In a moment she rose, picked up her handbag, and walked across the room.

"Where are you going?" His voice was sharp with resentment.

"Out on the terrace."

"Why can't I go? Why?"

"You stop that. Let go of me!" His fingernails scratched against the rough material of her blue jeans as he clung to her leg. The force of her push threw him off balance; he fell over backward onto the floor. Slowly he sat up, rubbing the back of his head, his face preparing for tears.

It was hot on the terrace; she lay on a couch with a wide canopy over it, writing a letter to her mother in Paris. Everything was fine at the nightclub where she worked, she said, and by summer she would surely have enough saved up to come home. In a little while she got up and went to the kitchen to get a glass of water. Vero, of course, would have rung for it, but she did not like to give orders to the servants; she merely let them know when she was ready to eat. With the cold water inside her, she returned to the terrace and finished her letter. Then she lay back and daydreamed a while, enjoying the first passage of the breeze that announced the possible advent of rain. When she went in for lunch, the cumulus clouds had advanced and expanded upward from all sides into what remained of the clear sky above.

She and Pepito had their sandwiches and salad at the table in the little bedroom. She had trained him to go directly from lunch to bed for his nap, principally because she herself could not do without a siesta at that hour. She sat on the couch reading for a few minutes after he was quiet, and then she stretched out and fell asleep.

The awakening from a heavy afternoon slumber is slow. She had seen Pepito go out of the room, she had heard the rain splattering on the balcony, and then she had been asleep again, perhaps for a long time. Next, Pepito was pushing his fingers into her neck. "Mommy! Mommy! Telephone!"

She stood up and staggered out into the kitchen. Paloma sat at the big table in the center, pointing to the corner of the room. She went over and picked up the receiver. It was Vero.

"What's the matter?" she said.

She could hear him laughing. "I just wanted to say Hi! See how you were. We're in Mi Cielo, you remember? The little cantina on the plaza. Got in here about fifteen minutes ago." They talked a little. Behind his voice, in the background, a church bell had begun to ring. She heard it booming through the air, above the noises of the bar. "See you around eight tomorrow night," he told her, and hung up.

She walked past Paloma, smiling self-consciously, and on into the library, where she stood gazing out at the terrace awash with rain under the dark sky. The air beyond the windows had become a gray expanse of falling water. "The rain is raining all around," she recalled. She had liked the verses as a child when she was learning English; they had made the rain into a friendly phenomenon. Here they meant nothing; it was a different kind of rain, violent and menacing.

In her head she could still hear the deep, full-throated sound of the church bell. But San Felipe was a village with one small church, and she knew the sound of its bell. It had a high, cracked ring like a metal pipe clanging, more like an alarm than a church bell. Vero was not in San Felipe at all. Where he might be she had no idea, but she knew it was not San Felipe Tonatan. She was thinking only that he had lied to her and she did not know why. I'm glad he won't marry me, she told herself.

14

HE GOT BACK A LITTLE AFTER SEVEN on Sunday evening. Luchita was sitting in Pepito's room reading when she heard him come in. As he entered the kitchen a moment later, he shouted to someone, "Go on outside! I'll be right out." Pepito had already rushed into the kitchen to meet him. She put the book down and stepped into the bathroom, where she stood before the mirror combing her hair. How am I going to look at him? she thought. It was as if she had been the one who had lied, rather than he. Then she heard him come into the bedroom, and she opened the door and walked toward him, still running the comb through her hair.

"Hi, Chita!" he cried, seizing her arm and spinning her around to kiss her. She submitted miserably, not looking into his eyes.

"How's everything?" he said.

She looked toward him but not at him. "Fine. Who's that with you?"

"Just Thorny."

"But I thought he was staying down at the ranch."

"He's going back down in a day or two." He let go of her, and she started back toward the bathroom.

"Where the hell's everybody?" he shouted from the kitchen. "Where's Manuel?"

"You said you'd come at eight, and I told them," she called. She could not hear the words of his reply, but their tone seemed to express dissatisfaction. A moment later she heard him putting bottles and glasses on a tray. Pepito was helping; he cried, "This one, Vero?"

"Pepito!" she called. When he appeared in the doorway she said, "Now you take your bath. I'll be back in fifteen minutes."

"I want to help Vero," he complained.

She seized him and pulled his shirt off over his head. Then she began to draw the water in the tub. "Where are you going?" he demanded. Thinking once again about the church bell, she did not answer. Because he was slow in undressing, she lent a hand; when he was naked, she patted him on the buttocks and pointed at the clock on the shelf. "Fifteen minutes," she repeated, and went out.

Vero was carrying the tray through the kitchen. "Bring some crackers and stuff," he told her.

It was warm on the terrace. Thorny stood at the edge, looking over the railing. The night sky was blue, crowded with stars, the mountains were black, and the long strands of street lamps were draped like cobwebs of light all across the valley below. Luchita walked over to the edge and leaned against the railing. "Hello," she said, looking toward Thorny. He was wearing a sweatshirt with a blazer over it, and his hair was rumpled.

"Oh," he said. "Hi, Luchita." he sighed deeply.

"You sick, or you just feel gloomy?" she inquired turning around and facing the terrace. He did not move.

"It isn't that, baby!" His voice was deep, and so husky as to be almost a whisper. "No, not gloomy! I just feel bad all over inside." He ran his hand vaguely down his torso.

"What'd you eat?" she demanded.

Vero came over with a drink for Thorny. "This'll help. Thorny's upset, that's all. We hit a dog and we heard it yelling while it died."

"Who was driving?" Vero glanced toward her, but

73

there was not enough light for her to see the expression on his face.

"*He* was driving! That's why he's upset," Vero said sharply; she could see that he did not want to talk about it, so she said no more. But she thought: He lets that maniac drive the station wagon.

Thorny turned to Luchita. "Baby, it was a terrible thing. A dog, yes; I know. But it's *life,* baby. It's life! Each time he screamed, a little of his life came out. And then it was gone. It made me feel bad, I don't know, to think that's all life is."

"Well, yes," said Luchita vaguely. "You can't tell. Maybe it isn't always that bad. Some people never even know they're dying."

"Or maybe it's worse," said Vero. "The dog was dead in five seconds. Who could ask for better than that?"

"You can't measure it!" Thorny cried in a stage whisper. "Five seconds, five years, forever! I swear to you, I'll *never* forget it!" He hesitated. Luchita took advantage of the break to observe, "Forever! Don't worry. *Your* life's not going to be so long."

Thorny had started to go on, but at the same instant Vero interrupted: "How's your drink? Can I fill it up?" He was squinting at Thorny's glass, trying to see the level in it. "What's the matter with you?" he cried. "Why aren't you drinking? Until you drink you're going to go on talking about it. Nobody wants to hear you talk about it." He said the last words a little more slowly. "You know?"

Thorny coughed, stood up straight, and drank.

"I think you got too much sun," Vero told him. "Why don't you sit down?"

Thorny finished his drink and held out his glass for more.

They listened while a plane flew over; when its roar had become only a reverberation passing farther down the valley, Thorny said, "Put on the new Cecil Taylor."

"Give me the glass." Vero filled it again, set the shaker down, and went inside. Luchita hummed for an instant. Then she said, "What's the matter with you?"

"I'm tired. The heat was rough." Faint strains of music began to come from behind the plants.

As Vero came back onto the terrace he called, "Thorny! Come and sit down. Or lie here and put your feet up."

Luchita went to the kitchen. Manuel and Paloma sat in a flood of fluorescent light at the table, talking. "*Buenas noches,*" they said.

Pepito was still in the tub, squeezing soapsuds from a washcloth. As she pulled out the plug and the water began to suck into the drainpipe, she heard the telephone ringing.

"Mommy, did Vero see any rattlesnakes?"

"I'll ask him," she said.

"Did he see any iguanas?"

"How do I know what he saw?" She was trying to get him dry with the damp towel. "Ask him tomorrow. They hit a dog on the way home. That's all he said."

"Oh!" Pepito was shocked.

"Thorny was driving," she went on quickly. "Vero couldn't do anything about it."

"Ah." He was relieved. "Vero wouldn't run over a dog, would he?"

She was sorry she had mentioned it. "It was an accident, Pepito. Get into your pajamas."

When Pepito was finally in bed and silenced, she went back out onto the terrace. Thorny lay in a swing couch, lightly swaying, listening to the jazz. He got up as she approached and put his forefinger conspiratorially to his lips. Taking her arm, he walked with her over to the parapet.

"Listen! Don't go inside. He's just had bad news. His mother's dead."

"His mother?" She was silent for a moment. Then, trying to unfasten his fingers from around her arm, she turned to face him, and cried, "Why shouldn't I go in?" She pulled away and ran a few steps, then walked the rest of the way to the library door. It was dark inside.

Vero lay on a couch staring upward, his hands behind his head. When she first went into the room she could scarcely see him. He turned toward her. "Did Thorny tell you?"

"Yes. I'm sorry, Vero. I'm very sorry."

"I just came in here for a few minutes. I wanted to be by myself."

"I know!" she cried, and, in spite of herself she reached down suddenly and seized his head in her two hands to kiss his forehead and cheeks. Then she stood up without saying any more and started to walk away.

"You and Thorny go ahead with dinner. I'll have something later."

At this she stood still and turned around. "You said he wasn't staying to dinner," she said in a stage whisper. "Why can't he go out?"

Vero looked at her in the way she did not like. "He's sick. Can't you see that? He should eat and go to bed. He's sleeping in the little bedroom tonight."

"Why can't he go home? It's not so far."

"Because I want him here in the morning, early."

She stepped nearer to the couch. "I'm not going to eat with him," she declared, still in her stage whisper.

He sprang up and seized her wrist, forcing her to be motionless for a moment. "Yes, you are." He looked at her steadily. "You're going to see that he gets to bed afterward, too. Jesus Christ! Is that so much to do for a man when his mother dies?"

Luchita shut her eyes and opened them. "I didn't mean to argue. I'm sorry. Lie down. I'll take care of him."

"Come back in when he's gone to bed. I'll be home by then."

"You're going out?"

"To the police station for a minute."

"Poor Vero," she said, shaking her head.

Manuel had set a formal table in the dining room. Apart from the candles, the only light came from behind the thicket of bamboo which filled one end of the room. While they were having soup they heard Vero go out. Luchita's spirits sank. Poor, poor Vero, she thought; the idea of having any sort of contact with the police filled her with dread. It did not occur to her to wonder why they wanted to see him.

Thorny, in spite of being a little drunk, still seemed depressed. In a way, that was fortunate, because he was less likely to talk. In any case, it was her duty to get through the meal somehow. When it was over, she reflected that he had not once spoken about the dog. And she hoped it was partly her doing. She wanted to help Vero however she could; to feel that she had done even that much made her happy.

They stood beside the table. "Well, good night," she said. "I know you want to go to bed. I've got to go and look at Pepito."

She did not hear any reply, but she turned and went through the pantry into the kitchen. When she came back with her cigarette-rolling machine, he had gone into his room.

Out on the terrace the jazz was still playing. She let

herself drop onto a mattress beside the swimming pool and began to make grifas to pass the time. The young frogs Vero had put into the smaller pool on the west terrace tried to croak, gave up, tried again. When she had five grifas prepared, she heard the library door shut.

"Vero?"

He came out and stood looking down at her, his hands in his pockets. "Well, that's that, at least," he said.

She moved over and touched the mattress beside her, and he sat down. "Wait," she said. She held a match to one of the cigarettes and handed it to him; then she lit another for herself and waited for him to speak. The minutes went past; the music played and the frogs chirped. When she had finished her cigarette she said, "What did the police want?"

He sighed. "They called about my mother. They wanted me to go down and look at something. I had to sign a paper."

"What for?"

"She died here. That's the point."

"Here!" Luchita's eyes opened very wide. She had seen many photographs of Vero's formidable mother; the thought of her being nearby, even in death, filled her with awe. (When she was really surprised, he thought fleetingly, she was cuter than at any other time. He wished he had waited until bedtime to tell her.)

"Well, not up here. Puerto Farol. I went down there to meet her." He flicked his butt into the air; it made a bright arc and disappeared over the edge of the building. Some day he would hit somebody and there would be trouble, she had repeatedly told him. Neither one spoke for a while. Then Luchita began excitedly, "But why'd you say you were going to the ranch? I knew you weren't in San Felipe. Why'd you lie to me?"

He hesitated. "I was going to surprise you," he said. "Meet her and bring her up."

Another lie, she thought. He would never even have let his mother know she existed, much less have brought her to the apartment while she was in it.

"You didn't meet her?"

"No," he said hopelessly.

She waited before she said, "But what happened?"

With a convulsive movement he stretched out beside her, looking toward her, his face twisted into what resembled an expression of agony.

"God! There was a fire! In the hotel! They brought up her gold mirror and some jewelry. I had to identify them." He was silent a while; then he turned slowly over onto his back. "It was a favor."

"What was a favor?"

"They let me do it here. Otherwise I'd have had to go all the way down to Puerto Farol."

"I see," she said with a sour smile. "Because you're you."

"It's a favor I appreciate," he said defensively.

"Yes. It wouldn't be the same down there a second time."

He looked at her.

"I mean, you had it the first time."

"Oh, God! *Had* it!" He put his arm over his eyes and left it there. "I got conscious around twilight, I remember, and we drove back into town. I know we went swimming. It was too late then even to go and see her at the Independencia. If I'd only met her at the boat she would never have been in the hotel at all."

"But what *happened?*" she said impatiently.

"Well, we were at one of those rat-hole cantinas on the waterfront. Some hacendero walks in. I've seen him here in town. He's telling us: *Hombre,* my finca's only six minutes from town, and so on. All right, we'll go to the finca. It's in the jungle. Not six minutes, of course. It's about twenty-five, a track full of mud and bushes, terrible! So we see the finca and his friends come in from other fincas and it's a big party. A long party. The boat anchored at seven the next morning, and I was asleep all day. I'd missed the boat anyway, and she was already in the hotel. I couldn't go and have her see me the way I was. I thought I'd wait and see her here."

"Oh, Vero! You didn't meet her, and then you just turned around and came back! That's terrible!"

"Ah," he said, almost with satisfaction. "You understand what I'm talking about, why I feel the way I do."

"Yes, but you shouldn't think it's your fault. That's not true, baby."

She lit another grifa and was silent while she smoked it. "It's lucky you didn't really care much about her," she said after reflection. "Think how much more you'd mind."

"My God! Your mother's your mother! Can't you see the shock would be just as great, no matter how you *felt* about her?"

Luchita shook her head in a matter-of-fact manner. "No. It would be worse. You don't know. You never loved your mother. You told me yourself."

"What's that got to do with it?" he cried. "It's much more than that. She's inside you! And when she dies something happens. It's the way life is made, that's all."

Luchita was thinking of her own mother in Paris. "Of course. But if you love her too, it's worse when she dies."

"You've got no mind," Vero said with finality.

The pile of records had given out; only the sound of the frogs remained.

"Thorny went to bed right after dinner," she told him.

"Did he go on with the dog business?"

"No," she said proudly. "He just ate his dinner."

He stood up and stretched. "He's tired out. It's a long drive up. You want to make me a sandwich?"

"You stay here," she said, happy to be put to use. "I'll bring everything."

"Bring it to bed. I'm going in."

15

WITH LUCHITA THERE WERE no scenes of flirtation, no voluptuous undressings; she kept him at arm's length until they were there, side by side, in the bed. Tenderness between them she could accept only as a by-product of love-making. Sometimes he tried merely looking at her steadily across the table, or from the other side of the room; she pretended not to notice, but always she ended by showing an emotional reaction of some kind, so that he felt he had at least partially imposed his will. However, she made it clear that she considered these tactics unfair, an invasion of her privacy. And yet, when the moment came, no one could be so carefree and passionate. It was an unalloyed blessing to be with her. Thus he was continually weighing the hindrances against the advantages. Making it possible for her to get back to Paris seemed safe enough: she was going back to face a degree of poverty she had not yet known. Soon she would be clamoring for a short vacation with him. At that time he would decide whether he really wanted her with him again or not, whether or not the intimacy he had to do without in his daily life was compensated for by the unusually high quality of her performance in bed.

Normally there were neither big days nor small ones in Grove's calendar. What he had had in mind when he had fitted together the various possibilities that would form and maintain his present life was an eternally empty schedule in which he would enjoy the maximum liberty to make sudden decisions. He wanted the basic pattern of each day to be as much as possible like that of the one before it. Friends and servants presented no problem; his father and Luchita, on the other hand, in all innocence did interfere occasionally with the smooth functioning of his personal pattern. This was to be expected: the one supplied him with money and the other with pleasure. But as a permanent situation it was unacceptable. To have moral support he had encouraged Thorny to forsake Canada and come to live in the capital. Thorny was a ruin, but so had he been during their student days together, and since he was quick, intuitive, and appreciative of every facet of Grove's personality (without, however, being easy to manipulate), it was natural for Grove to have decided to make him available. He wanted to have him around—in the background, but nearby. Each time old Señor Soto threatened to precipitate a crisis, or the struggle with Luchita grew too acute to go on bearing without a hiatus, he would get hold of Thorny, and they would go off somewhere together. Because Thorny's monthly income was barely sufficient to pay for a cheap apartment and the simple food he ate in it, he was always ready to accept an invitation; the more involved the expedition and the longer it took, the more money he had left when he returned to wait for his next check to arrive from home. Although Señor Soto and Luchita seldom were of the same opinion on anything, both objected strongly to Thorny, and for the same reasons. "Can't you see when a man is taking advantage of you?" demanded old Señor Soto. It seemed to him that Thorny's influence was not a civilizing one in Grove's life. And Luchita: "That bum! He thinks this is a hotel. You encourage him."

The present project had presented itself rather suddenly and was not a direct outgrowth of domestic pressures. It was only about three weeks earlier that the idea had occurred to him. There was work being done on the ranch at San Felipe. He would tell Luchita he was going there, and instead slip down to Puerto Farol with Thorny for a day or two.

The trip could be successful only if he made it in a state of absolute calm. This tranquility was something he had studied to attain. It was fairly easy: using an empirical system of autohypnosis he obliged himself to believe that the present was already past, that what he felt himself to be doing he had already done before, so that present action became merely a kind of playback of the experience. By ridding himself of all sense of immediacy with his surroundings, he was able to remain impervious to them.

However, when he had set the calming apparatus in motion he became untalkative. Thorny knew all about it; he had noticed that the functioning of the device made Grove silent and morose. It was an unimportant concomitant of the process whereby Grove assumed certain attributes of superhumanity; there was no question of his infallibility at such times. Knowing that the master was going to be operating under pressure, Thorny was prepared for an unpleasant journey.

They drove down the highway under the hanging orchids, a *mejorana* wailing into their faces from the radio panel. The day was clear, the air light. When they got into the lowlands the giant sky turned gray. There were stretches where the road was narrow and curving, and the vegetation, reaching out from both sides, hit the car and scraped along its body. The back of Grove's shirt was wet and cold; he turned and saw the sweat running down the plastic fabric of the cushion. The hot filthy villages went past, the forest between them black and rotting.

Now that the trip was all over, he lay on the fur under the frozen menace of the plants, his hands behind his head, triumphant at having managed so far not to have reviewed even once any of its details. When the telephone call came from the police he thought only of how he was going to behave in front of Luchita. "Tell her, but keep her away from me for a while if you can," he said to Thorny; but he was not surprised when she had sought him out immediately, as soon as she had heard. He had not had time; he had had to play it by ear. Still he did not think he had done too badly, and when he returned from his visit to police headquarters he resolved to go ahead in the same improvised vein of behavior. It seemed to him that tonight could prove to be one of their really good nights; her tender outburst upon hearing about his mother suggested that.

In the dimness of the room, while Luchita looked for food in the kitchen, he lay on the bed and considered his reflection. He had installed electrically adjustable mirrors in place of the headboard and footboard—ridiculous gadgets that he sometimes set up to amuse Luchita during their bed games. Since her return from Señor Guzman's he had been prudent enough to refrain from using them. Tonight?

There was no mystery; it was perfectly clear to him, as he followed the line of his cheeks and chin down to his neck and shoulders, why any girl would be happy to be in bed with him. He grinned lasciviously into the mirror of the footboard. Faintly he heard the kitchen sounds. It was his habit to stay away from that part of the house. In spite of all the white enamel and conspicuous hygiene, there was always a hint of the sour smell of garbage out there, as though rotten papaya rinds might be lying behind the doors. And then there was the boy.

After he had eaten, many grifas were smoked, the Baluba drummers played behind the bamboo plants, the mirrors tilted and flashed, the night was transformed. Eden on all sides, with him at the heart of it.

Although he was aware that all was well because he was in the big bed and had Luchita with him, pressed against him all the way down to his faraway feet, nevertheless he dreamed he was lying face down on a narrow cot. The two glass walls on either side of his mattress met in a point, not far from the pillow where his head lay. It was like having a bed that was fitted into the prow of a ship, save that he was poised high above an illimitable city whose streets were so far below that the traffic which filled them was soundless.

Attached to the cot by a complicated chromium fixture was an outsize Easter egg made of sparkling pink and white sugar crystals, and lighted from within. He peered into the lens at the end of the egg: a television program was being flashed across a surface which, thanks to the extraordinary amplifying power of the tiny lens, proved to be an enormous screen in a darkened hall full of spectators.

He had got in at the beginning of a program. As the

music blared, he raised himself slightly off the cot and glanced behind him. Through the glass walls at the footboard he saw the actual hall below; the glass cage was one of several hundred such cells, a honeycomb of niches built into the walls of the auditorium. Now that he was sitting up, he felt dizzy. He lay down again and tried to make himself comfortable. Before adjusting the angle of the egg to his eye, he examined a group of three small press-buttons arranged in a vertical row at the side of the lens. Keeping his finger on the top button, he arranged the angle of the egg and peered through the lens once more. Credits were still unfolding on the screen. As the first image came on, he pressed the button.

Immediately he knew that the little sugar egg was a priceless gadget. There was a slight whirring, as of a generator being set in motion, and the already extremely dim lights in the auditorium were further lowered momentarily. Then they slowly returned to their former intensity. The important point was that the machine gave him the illusion of actually standing in the auditorium. It occurred to him that it would be a triumph if he could arrange to unscrew the egg from the fixture and take it with him when he left.

It was then that he felt terror, sat up, and lifted his hand above his head. His fingers touched the glass before he had stretched his arm very far. It was a box, this chamber where he lay. He was enclosed; there was no air-conditioning panel. And he was convinced that the air was already growing heavy and foul; he imagined he could detect the stink of his own breath. He lay down again, vastly depressed but in the particular state of paralyzed acceptance which the dreamer does not combat. There was a faint but distinct smell of ozone coming, as in a fine spray, from the direction of the egg. The first button was still down. Suddenly he understood that the buttons constituted an escape; they provided an exit to be used in emergencies. He looked again into the egg and straightway had the illusion of being in the auditorium, standing back in the dark at the head of an interminable aisle. Beyond was the screen. Staring up at the great bright rectangle now for the first time, he saw the face of a well-known, faded, middle-aged actress; he could not remember her name. The thirty-foot-high figure stood there sadly, her hair disheveled, in the pathetic role of a distraught matron. There was a strong flavor of remonstrance in her voice. He noticed that she had made even the single word *yes* sound recriminatory.

Repelled by the character she was playing but fascinated by the quality of the acting, he began to walk down the aisle. An end seat was empty. As he sat down he was aware of a certain agitation in the audience. The woman on the screen was pointing with her forefinger; suddenly he saw her in the flesh, tiny and down at one side of the screen, with brilliant spotlights focused on her head. He watched the small bright figure raise its arms as if welcoming the audience, and he had an unreasonable conviction that things were going to go badly from this moment on. Stealthily he stretched out his hand and felt along the armrest of his seat. The top button was still depressed; he waited an instant, trying to understand what the actress was saying. It was a complaint; she sobbed, her words were unintelligible and the inflections of her voice were growing hysterical. And constantly the music was rising in volume and dramatic intensity. If it went on, he would be paralyzed, unable even to push a button. Carefully he moved his finger a half-inch along the surface of the armrest until it touched the second button. He hesitated an instant, and then he pushed it down with a click.

The actress screamed and twitched, as though a powerful electric current had been sent through her. Immediately he knew that something terrible was going to happen: he had set the wrong forces in motion. He raised his head to stare at the screen. There was no element of surprise in his emotions as he watched the transformation take place—only a dull horror at the inevitability of it. The woman's features faded, slid away, melted swiftly, and the face took on its true identity, the one he now knew he had been expecting from the start—that of his mother.

Even here, he thought miserably. What does she want here? Now he watched both the screen and the doll-like figure in the flesh-colored pool of light at the foot of it, feeling his heart beat faster. With her "jolly" look, which never once had fooled him even as a small child, she began to talk as though she were addressing one of her clubs, as though the audience were made up only of women. Underneath the jovial flesh was the supremely calculating consciousness, the dark destroying presence. No matter what part she was playing (for her role depended upon her audience), to him her basic expression was always the same, cunning and omniscient, with an undertone of implicit menace, as though it had been universally conceded that woman's state, entailing persecution and suffering, included her right to seek vengeance.

"I came here," she was saying (he grew tense) . . . "to see my son. I thought they might be working on him tonight." Her smile was an apology for the boundlessness of human frailty; he looked straight into its amplified folds on the screen as he rose to his feet and felt himself dissolving in horror. If he went up the aisle they would stop him. He crossed over and entered a row of seats, squeezing himself along in front of the seated spectators toward an exit door near the end. There was a certain amount of whispered protest as he pushed his way through, but he felt certain he had not been identified. When he got to the side aisle he flung the door open and in spite of himself turned for a last glimpse of the screen. She was looking straight at him. That means she's looking at the camera, he reminded himself.

"Grover!" Her voice was cool and imperious; it became contemptuous as she asked, "Have you finished?"

With all his might he screamed back, "No!" and felt the hall tremble with the force of his cry. As he began to run along the dark corridors he thought, She knows about the glass room upstairs. She's the one who had me committed.

The backstage world was a labyrinth of narrow stairways and dingy storerooms. The place was empty of people, but he had no idea where he was going, and it seemed to him that he could hear a murmur of disturbance back in the auditorium. And he kept running, through the corridors, up circular staircases, down interior fire escapes and along galleries that overhung unlighted depths, increasingly convinced that this was a flight to save his life; by rising from his seat in the audience he had in some way interfered with institutional processes. He would be caught and punished. At that point Luchita coughed and moved her hand roughly along his thigh.

The sweetness of the night came pouring in from all sides. The fountain gurgled on the terrace, there was a slight sound of wind in the leaves, and somewhere a motorcycle labored upward from the valley below. Luchita moved into a new position and went on breathing regularly. He lay completely still, feeling shame because his heart still pounded so wildly.

Still without moving, in a half-sleep, he tried to reconstruct the world of the little nightmare: he had to understand whatever he was afraid of. Was it possible that even knowing she was dead, he was not going to be able to diminish the dread of her that was still there inside him? He listened to the fountain, to the wind below in the pines. His heart went on beating oppressively; in an effort to calm it, he tried taking deep and regular breaths.

He had backed out of the garage and was sitting at the wheel of the Cadillac, ready to be off, but his mother had appeared in the driveway and now leaned against the car door, her head inside, and she was talking. "Just remember, when you're out on that highway, the difference between the brake and the accelerator is the difference between life and death. Will you try to remember that, just for me?"

The words made him squirm. "For God's sake, Mother!"

"If only you weren't always on the defensive," she said wistfully, adding, as if to herself, "Of course, with no father—"

In simulated anger he had started up, so that she nearly lost her balance. This had taken days to smooth over, but he knew it had been the correct move. The inevitable pattern of his life had been one of exploiting the enmity between her and his father; yet in the presence of each he had preserved what appeared to be a basic loyalty toward the other. If he came back to the capital after a visit to Montreal and described his mother's civic campaigns and her women's club banquets, he was careful to include details which he knew would infuriate

Señor Soto, who had his own Latin ideas on female behavior; and before he went back to Montreal he made lists of seemingly anodyne details which had to be innocently incorporated into his conversations with his mother. It was necessary to hint that Señor Soto's house might be one of the last places on earth where a mother would want her son to be. If there were any overt criticism from her, however, he assumed a disturbed air and begged her gently, "Please . . . Please!"

The winter when he was sixteen, Señor Soto had tried to persuade him to go with him to mass on Sunday; in an offhand, dogmatic fashion he told him that the only way to be free in life was to adhere so strictly to an orthodoxy that everything save the spirit became a matter of reflex. Grove had given a good deal of thought to this; it seemed a viable technique, providing you found a valid orthodoxy. Later in the year he expounded the theory to his mother.

"You're not turning out to be a fanatic, I hope!" she cried, going on ruefully, "I don't understand it. You don't get this taste for excess from my side of the family. That goes with the Church. You can smell it a mile away. I thought you had more balance."

"It's a question of discipline," he told her.

She shook her head slowly back and forth. "Don't let him rope you into the Church, Grove. I warn you. It's fatal."

"You know he's an agnostic," he said quietly.

"Is that what he claims to be?" She looked up, startled. That had done it; later in the day she suggested buying a motorboat and spending the autumn at Percé. "I don't have to have a boat," he told her. "Don't spend the money." She had bought the boat and they had gone to gether up to the Gaspé. The college propaganda began again during this long holiday. She wanted to enter him at McGill the following year. Grove, knowing that he was in the position of the head of a neutralist state, instead spent the winter with his father in the beach house at Puerto Pacífico, persuaded that the following summer would bring forth something more substantial than a motorboat. Señor Soto's opinion of the value of a college education was very low; he wanted to give him practical experience in administering one of the haciendas. "But if you want to try it, you've got one of the oldest universities in the world right here in the capital."

"I don't want to try it!" Grove told him. "I just want to keep the peace."

"Don't let yourself be pressured," his father advised him.

His moves had all been correct. Summer brought the Cadillac, a bonus for agreeing to live with his mother and attend the University; he would have been happier if a truck had not backed into it one night after he had parked it in front of a roadhouse. It was more than he could do to face her with the news. He had bought a plane ticket to Panama and gone directly up to Puerto Pacífico. The end of his academic career had not shaken his mother so deeply as the fact that he had left without letting her know, without giving her a chance to say goodbye. In spite of all the times he had seen her since, even now he found himself frowning there in the dark as he recalled it; but the feeling of guilt could no longer be reshaped into anger, because there was nothing left to fear. It was long past, he told himself, and it was something she should have expected, in any case. When the daylight began to show from the terrace he fell back into sleep.

16

IN THE MORNING the first sound Luchita heard was the splashing of water in the swimming pool. She reached down and pulled the sheet up over her, for she was naked. Then she felt tentatively along the mattress beside her for Vero. His place was empty. She went back to sleep. Later she woke to see him dressing; he seemed to be in a great hurry. Presently he stepped over to the bed and spoke to her, and she came really awake. He had put on a business suit.

"What time is it?" she asked.

"Ten to eight."

"What's wrong? What are you doing up so early?"

"I've got to go out. I'll be back for lunch."

"You look high." She squinted at him.

"You never heard of feeling good in the morning?" He pulled down the sheet and set to tickling her savagely. She struggled, buried her face in the pillows to stifle her screams, tried unsuccessfully to kick him. At the moment when she felt she could stand it no longer, he stopped and stood up.

"You be here for lunch, though," he said, adjusting his tie. "You can help me."

She had yanked the sheet up around her neck. "My God, what'd they lay on you, anyway?" she cried.

"Go back to sleep," he told her.

Just before lunch was ready he returned, still in a state of excitement, and began to rush noisily around the kitchen. Luchita came out of Pepito's room. He was putting ice cubes into a bowl. Leaning against the refrigerator, smoking, she listened to him describe the visit to the bookshop. At length she said impassively, "You like her?"

"I'm not planning to screw her, if that's what you mean."

She shrugged and went back into the bedroom. Over lunch they discussed the morning visitor. "You were right not to come out if you were going to look like that," he told her. "You'll meet her tomorrow night. If you can arrange to wear something else instead of those Levis, I'd appreciate it."

"Whatever you like," she said meekly; she had determined to make an attempt to please him during this period. She waited, then said, "Where's Thorny?"

"He went out to Los Hermanos. He won't be back till late tonight."

"That's a good place for him," she declared. "I wish he'd stay there. I'm going down to the movies with Pepito."

After lunch, instead of taking his accustomed siesta, he shut himself into the library with a notebook and a sheaf of papers. When Luchita had been gone for a half hour or so, he switched on a tape recorder and listened. Here he had been preparing one of his discussions with Luchita. Often he improvised these one-sided conversations, recorded them, and then wrote out notes on the more convincing passages. Using these, he plotted the course of a verbal procedure from which he allowed himself almost no deviation when the moment came for actual speaking.

"All right. You don't know me. You always say you have no idea what I'm like. But at least you know what I'm *not* like. I'm not like most people. I want the same thing, always. I don't like changes. You ought to know. You've checked up. You know I never brought anybody back nights, before you came. I want you here next to me when I wake up. That's not so hard to understand, is it?"

He reversed the tape to its beginning, set the microphone on the coffee table, and began to record over the month-old monologue. For an instant he stood staring down at the slowly turning reels. "Day," he said tentatively, as if the uttering of the word might effect some palpable change in the room. "Wait while I get a cigarette."

When he came in from the terrace he lay down on the divan facing the table. He spoke for a while; his voice was gentle, his inflections those of one seeking agreement at the most basic level of rationality. The pauses for her hypothetical replies were brief. He lit another cigarette and balanced it on the edge of the ashtray. The smoke rose in a long line, straight into the air. It was too soon for the late-afternoon wind to have arrived. He watched the little cylinder of white paper with its thin blue column of smoke, and thought, If it were now. This was a recurrent fantasy, an obsessive pastime in which he often indulged during periods of stress. If he should vanish at this moment and *they* should come, wanting to learn about him, what would they find? One British cigarette, burning, balancing on the edge of the ashtray, the tape recorder turning, carrying only silence to the tape. They could talk with the servants and with one retarded Cuban girl (Luchita knew nothing about him and would be hostile anyway), and they would get nowhere. Making himself into one of them for the instant and generously granting that one an intelligence akin to his own, he ran his eye approvingly over the nearest row of books. *Ferien am Waldsee, Erinnerungen eines Überlebenden.*

L'Enfer Organisé. Netchaiev. Cybernation and the Corporate State. L'Univers Concentrationnaire. Auschwitz, Zeugnisse und Berichte. Even though the man were an enemy, for they were all enemies, those who would come after his disappearance to verify his essence, the inspector would be profoundly impressed by the sum of the evidence. The report could read: "This kind of genius for achieving total perfection has no application in an era of collective consciousness." Imagining his own nonexistence never failed to stimulate him; he continued to speak, now in an even calmer voice.

"But if we're going to be friends, you've got to know me completely. Isn't that always the case if there's going to be understanding? You've got to know what I'm all about and why I'm the way I am. If we're going to talk to each other we've got to be in the same psychic room, as it were. You say I'm difficult. I'm like anyone else. But I care a great deal about the truth. It's hard to come by and it makes trouble, but it's worth it. Or don't you admit that?" He looked quizzically at the microphone standing on its chromium tripod; often it reminded him of a machine gun. *Ametralladora, modelo bolsillo,* he thought, and smiled at it. Then he got up and walked to the bar by the window, threw a proprietary glance at the city shining below in the sudden gold light of sunset beneath the storm clouds, and poured out a glass of cherry brandy. He began to talk on his way back to the table, walking slowly, holding the glass at eye level, staring into it. "We're machines for realizing the inconceivable, and we go on living like animals, being subjective, with personal tastes and preferences. In India, you know, there are people who claim that love is obscene unless both parties are so conscious of what they are doing—I mean so absolutely aware of themselves and each other

96

during sex—that they can concentrate on God all the way through to the end, both of them. What it really means is that you've got to be both intelligent and shameless. But the Hindus always turn out to be practical." He sipped from his glass. "I believe they've hit it. Sex will never be any good until we're free. At least free enough to be able to focus on God while we're doing it." He laughed self-consciously. "You can see that it could be a great discipline, just in order to improve the quality of the experience. The whole point of sex is that it should be as good as possible."

At this point he imagined her saying, "Were we talking about sex?" She had a dry authoritative way of cutting a conversation short; she allowed the traffic to circulate only along the main highway. This was a hindrance, but stupid women are more difficult to manage than bright ones. And it occurred to him that the school-principal element in her character might be a sign that she was already ruined for unashamed love-making.

It would be impossible, without being explicit, to convey to her a sense of the necessity of an immediate decision; he could not hope for that. If when he finished talking to her he could not be certain that he had won, he would give up the sex project entirely. He knew just where in the garden at Los Hermanos the talk would take place. By a circular pool there was a wide balustrade from which you looked down across the terraced land to the tangled forest beyond. A relaxing landscape, made voluptuous by moonlight.

A violent rainstorm broke while Luchita and Pepito were in the theater. When they came out, it had passed, but the streets had become rushing brooks. Before she could find a taxi, Pepito had managed to step into the water and get wet as far up as his waist.

"Oh, Pepito! You're so stupid!"

"I like to be wet," he said. "It feels good."

When she had got him into dry clothes it was nearly dinnertime. She walked out onto the terrace and looked through the door into the library. Vero was there, sitting at the desk under the light, writing. She stepped inside. "You still busy?" she asked him.

He looked up. "That's right." He yawned and stretched. "I'll finish later, before I go to bed."

After dinner he went into the library, shut the doors, and was back with his papers. Luchita wandered from the terrace into the bedroom and back a few times. It was one of those nights, frequent at the end of the dry season, when there seemed to be no air anywhere. From the library she heard the distant clicking of the typewriter. She went into the bedroom and stood in front of the mirror. Whatever he was doing, she reflected, it was better than thinking about his mother; also she had an irrational conviction that his work had some hidden connection with the eventual purchase of her ticket to Paris. She lit a grifa and pulled on it a few times. Suddenly she went to the library door. She hesitated an instant and threw it open.

"I've got to have some music!" she cried. "I can't just sit in here alone with nothing."

He did not look up. "Play it on the terrace and keep it low."

She stood there with her eyes fixed on the bright desk as if it might help her to divine what was written on the papers in front of him. Very slowly she swung the door, and still watched through the crack before she shut it entirely, taking care not to let the knob click when she lifted her hand from it.

17

THE MOTOR ROARED as they went up the mountain. The valley below was almost sunk in shadow. Dr. Slade sniffed the air noisily. "Now, if you could make a perfume that smelled like *that!*" he exclaimed. He sat up straight at each hairpin curve and peered over the drop. The day of visits to parks and palaces had been tiring; his nerves were a little on edge. It was pleasant when they got to the top and parked on level ground in front of the apartment house.

They came out of the elevator, were in a patio where a fountain played above a pool. There was a girl standing in an arched doorway, very young and extraordinarily beautiful. In her white gown she looked to Mrs. Slade just about old enough to write her first love letter.

"Here's Luchita!" cried Señor Soto. "This is Luchita. Mrs. Slade. Dr. Slade."

"Come in," said Luchita. "Please come in."

"This room! It's a work of art!" Mrs. Slade raised her arms upon entering it again, and turned to her husband.

"Yes, yes. It certainly is," he agreed, standing still an instant to look around, and then following Señor Soto across the room and out onto the terrace. The air in there had seemed stuffy; there had been a faint animal smell in it, or, if not exactly animal, something he connected with "native" life. He could not identify it, but he knew it was surprising to find the smell here in this apartment.

"Yes, this is quite an amazing place you've got here, Señor Soto. Quite amazing." He felt a bit insincere as he said the words; it looked to him more like an overpoweringly elegant hotel than a home. A hotel or a department store. "Yes. It's very fine indeed." He turned to the sunset over the valley. "What a sight!"

Señor Soto smiled. "Yes. Sunset up here is something big. Wait. I'll get you a drink. What is it?"

"Scotch and soda."

Dr. Slade watched the young man as he walked away across the terrace. He frowned. The all-enveloping charm of his young host made him uneasy; without hesitation he rejected it. There was no chance of its being real. And he thought with annoyance that it was typical of Day to be taken in by such a couple. She could disregard all the pretense and vulgarity, if only she found them "fun." He walked back toward the doorway. She and the girl were sitting among mountains of fur-covered cushions; each had a cocktail glass in her hand. Señor Soto appeared, carrying drinks. He joined Dr. Slade in the doorway, and they remained there talking.

Mrs. Slade was being a guest. "I think this apartment is the most beautiful thing I've ever seen!"

"I'm just invited here," Luchita said, looking downward. "I live in Paris."

Mrs. Slade shut her lips together and rearranged her skirt over her knees. "Paris. I don't think I could live there. The traffic."

"I hate it here," said Luchita.

"Really?" She laughed uneasily, and with a glance took in the entire room. "Oh, come on. You don't like living in this incredible place?"

"I'm going to Paris soon. The people in these small towns are lousy."

"Yes, I see how they could be," she began uncertainly, thinking of the overdressed crowd in the hotel dining

100

room. "But really it's a very pleasant little city. We've been sightseeing today, so I have a fresh eye."

"Yes. I suppose it looks pretty to tourists," Luchita said thoughtfully.

"I don't think you could call us exactly tourists," Mrs. Slade said. "We just move around where we please, when we please. It's the only way to do it. Group travel's a degradation. The whole point is to be free. Not to have to make reservations ahead of time."

Luchita was not listening; she did, however, hear the last sentence, and it struck no sympathetic chord in her. "I like my reservations a long time before, I can tell you."

Mrs. Slade was thrown off balance. "Oh, well, of course . . ." She laughed, not knowing what she had intended to say, and then smiled in order to camouflage her scrutiny of reappraisal. She looked carefully into Luchita's eyes, and had the peculiar feeling that she was studying an alien species. Señor Soto and Taylor stood talking in the doorway, with the sunset behind them.

"It's getting brighter every minute!" she cried.

Señor Soto came over and squatted, facing her.

"I was reading some Javanese poems today," he told her. "And I came across a line that won't go away."

"Javanese poetry?"

"That's right. 'The moon is more splendid than a young girl who looks the other way.' You like it?"

"I'm not quite sure I understand it," she said evenly, as if she thought that might stop him.

He laughed, took her arm, and pulled her up. "Come outside and look at the sunset while I explain it." They passed in front of Dr. Slade as they went through the doorway.

"Do you want to see the sunset again?" said Luchita, smiling at Dr. Slade.

"No, I don't think I do."

"Why don't you come and sit down?"

She told him about her father's orchestra, and how they all had left Havana and gone to Paris and become very successful, so that she had had many fine clothes. But then her father had died and the orchestra had broken up, and her mother had had to lend many of the musicians money to get back to Havana, until they had become extremely poor, which was why she must get to Paris soon. "How do I even know if my mother is alive?" she cried.

"I should think you'd want to go back," he said in tones of concern. "I shouldn't think it would be much pleasure being on vacation if you're going to worry like this. It'll wear you down."

"I know."

"You'd better go soon," he said, meaning to sound fatherly; he suspected that she thought him senile.

Earlier in the evening Luchita had smoked a great deal, and was now so bewitched by the sound of her own story that she was aware of him only in his capacity as listener. Overstimulated, he thought, but not drunk; she had not touched her drink since Day had gone out onto the terrace. Suddenly she stopped talking and stood up. "I have to go and feed my son," she told him, and went out of the room.

Mrs. Slade had been standing with her host, looking out over the darkening valley, while he explained the several possible meanings of the line of poetry; she had no idea what he was talking about, because she was not listening. When she thought he had finished, she said, "That girl. Your guest. She's a real crazy kid, isn't she?"

He frowned. "It's very hard to know what she's like," he said reflectively.

"Oh, come! You must be in a position to manage *that* much!"

"It's not exactly what you think," he protested.

"God forbid!" she exclaimed, laughing.

He looked at her but said nothing, and she felt rebuffed. After a moment he went on. "For one thing, she lives on grass. You know, marijuana." He gave it the Spanish pronunciation.

"Can't you stop her? Haven't you any influence at all over her? She's so young to be ruining her life."

"It keeps her quiet," he said, laughing. "I'm not one for trying to change people."

Mrs. Slade frowned at him. "I'm afraid I could never sit by and watch someone I cared about, or *didn't* care about, even, destroy himself, and not at least make an effort to do something about it."

"You see," he said with great seriousness, "I haven't noticed any signs of self-destructiveness in Luchita, so it's hard to know what to say."

Mrs. Slade was suddenly prim. "Of course, it's none of my business."

"Let me bring you another," he said, reaching for her glass. She held on to it and shook her head. "I think I'd like to go in. It's getting cool out here."

Inside she found Dr. Slade sitting alone, absently running his fingers back and forth over the chinchilla spread on which he sat. "Oh! I thought you were talking to—" she hesitated— "the young lady."

"She's gone to feed her child," he said very distinctly, and she glanced at him to see his face. At the same instant he looked up at her, and she recognized the glint of accusation in his eyes. It was the expression he always wore when he wanted to remind her that he was suffering for her sake. He was bored with the girl and bored with Señor Soto, and it was her fault. She walked over and sat down beside him.

"It's lovely, isn't it?" she said, watching his hand smooth the fur.

"Lovely?" he said blankly.

The telephone rang. They heard Señor Soto say, "*Diga. Quién habla?*" and then go into English. Shortly after that he laughed. "I thought he'd want to. Well, all I can do is ask. Put Dirk on." He called across the room. "Dr. Slade! Will you talk to this friend of mine who's sick? He's coming to the phone now. I told him you were here."

Dr. Slade stood up, and was already walking toward the end of the room where Señor Soto stood with the receiver in his hand. "Why, of course. Gladly."

And so it was that less than five minutes later he found himself, with considerable relief, back in the car with Señor Soto, breathing the resinous evening air as they sped around the mountain in the direction of an upland valley.

"It's only as far as Los Hermanos, if that means anything to you. A little place about twenty minutes out. He's going to appreciate this more than you realize."

"I can't do anything for him, you understand. I haven't been a practicing physician in a good many years."

"No, but it'll boost his morale. He's an American, after all, so he only really trusts American doctors."

"Naturally," said Dr. Slade.

They went over a mountain pass. Without warning, the air was bitterly cold. The stars that shone in the still twilit sky seemed abnormally large and bright. Then the road pirouetted downward through matted forest into a warm, windless valley choked with lush vegetation.

"This is Los Hermanos," Señor Soto said, turning to see his guest's reaction to the inglorious line of thatched huts and adobe boxes going past on each side of the road. Ever since they had come into the valley there had been the constant croaking of frogs; even in the middle of the town it was still audible.

Dr. Slade did not give any visible sign that he had heard the words. He was looking up the grass-filled streets as they passed them. Each one had two or three arc lights where the children clustered. Beyond, in the background, was the darkness of the forest. He had the impression that each street, as they approached it and he saw the swiftly changing vignette of light and shadow, was concerned intimately with some part of him, that he had even lived here for great periods of time. And the thought occurred to him that this shabby little town was very likely a model village in the eyes of the Creator; this was probably the kind of place in which all men were meant to live. The sound of the frogs could have been going on since the beginning of life. Another thing: he had begun to be aware of a general discomfort; there was a heaviness in him. He shut his eyes. I've caught a chill, he thought. At that moment the car swung off the highway onto a dirt road. Soon jungle arched above them. Señor Soto drove slowly, now and then turning to look at the doctor. The noise made by the frogs and insects was tremendous.

Slumping in his seat, Dr. Slade looked up at the vines and branches above his head. Then he shut his eyes again. What he had perceived was too unpleasant. Only a moment before, he had made the discovery that the frogs were aware of being a chorus; they sang together in rhythm. Then, for the fraction of a second, looking up at the chaos of vegetation overhead, he had very clearly seen each bough and leaf pulsating with the frogs, in exactly the same rhythmic patterns. He folded his hands over his chest and sighed.

"You need a jeep for this," said Señor Soto.

"Yes," he answered absently. Recovering for a second, he thought, "Alcohol is dangerous at this altitude," and resolved to drink more slowly.

The car stopped. An Indian in overalls, with a rifle in one hand, swung the big gate inward. "*Sí señor*," he said, and they drove on through a garden. Squat palms lined the driveway. Ahead, a car was parked beside a great dark mass of bushes. Señor Soto eased in beside it and shut off the motor. The frogs were singing here too, and the noise was as loud as it had been back in the jungle. The headlights went off; the garden glowed with impossible colors in the dim starlight.

"This has got to be done," Dr. Slade said to himself. He reached out his hand and pressed the door handle, took two or three steps on the spongy grass, and raised his head. In front of him, not three feet away, there was a face—a muzzle, rather, for it surely belonged to an animal—looking at him with terrible intensity. It was unmoving, fashioned from a nameless, constantly dripping substance. Unmoving, yet it must have moved, for now the mouth was much farther open; long twisted tendons had appeared in each cheek. He watched, frozen and unbelieving, while the whole jaw swiftly melted and fell away, leaving the top part of the muzzle intact. The eyes glared more savagely than before; they were telling him that sooner or later he would have to pay for having witnessed that moment of its suffering. He took a step backward and looked again. There were only leaves and shadows of leaves—no muzzle, no eyes, nothing. But the leaves were pulsating with energy. At any moment they could swell and become something other than what they were.

"The door's around this way," a man's voice was saying. He looked, and could see no one. Slowly he squatted and sat down on the grass with his knees up, his arms folded around them and his head bent over facing the earth.

"Is anything wrong?" the voice asked.

"I don't—" He could not say it. The frogs' song slurred upward, over and over again. If there was a person nearby, it could only be a stranger.

The stranger was pulling him to his feet. It was not really any harder to walk than it had been to sit doubled over listening to the frogs. A part of him had been shut out and was trying in anguish to join the other part that was shut in, but there was not even a way of thinking about it. A gill-like orifice gaped on each side of his neck; he could feel the pair of them opening and shutting regularly.

"You were out in the sun today. No?"

This was a red jungle. There were floor lamps and rugs in the clearings, and rows of books back in the shadows. The wilderness was peopled, but the men were all strangers. They held a cup of something hot to his lips. "Can you drink this?"

"I'm all right." This was what one was supposed to say, and he said it; yet he was aware of the outside world rushing away, retreating before the onslaught of a vast sickness that welled up inside him, and he knew that soon there would be only the obscene reality of himself, trapped in the solitary chambers of existence.

18

After Vero and the old American had left, Luchita went around turning on all the lights in the apartment. "Sometimes I like lots of light," she explained. "You know, it makes me feel something's happening." She returned to the couch and lay back on the cushions with her hands behind her head.

"Yes, I suppose."

"Do you ever feel nothing is happening?"

Mrs. Slade looked at her disapprovingly. "I don't think I do. No."

Luchita sat partially up. "You mean you've *never* bumped into it?"

But Mrs. Slade did not seem to want to talk about that. "How old is your child?" she asked her.

"You want to see him?"

Now she looked happier. "Oh, yes!"

Luchita led her to the little bedroom where Pepito was spooning up his food.

"Pepito, this is Mrs. Slade."

He smiled and continued to eat.

They went back into the library. There was no light left in the sky. "How long do you think they'll be gone?" Mrs. Slade asked her; she did not find it reassuring to have been left alone with this strange girl.

"They'll be back soon. It's not far," said Luchita. Part of helping Vero was to keep this not very friendly young woman occupied while he was gone. She spoke once again of Paris.

Suddenly Mrs. Slade cut her short. "Your husband,"

she said, and shook her head back and forth anxiously. "Where is he?"

"I've never been married," Luchita said earnestly, as if astonished that anyone should have supposed such a thing. "And *he's* not going to marry me!" She laughed to make it clear that she was free of illusions.

Mrs. Slade was silent. After a while she said, "Who's the boy's father?"

"Some English guy," Luchita said indifferently.

"Won't he help?"

"It was somebody in England. I don't know who," she explained. "Pepito looks English, too, a little. Don't you think?"

This could only be purposeful, thought Mrs. Slade. The girl was trying to provoke a reaction; she would not oblige her by supplying one. "There are so many different English types," she said evenly. "You can't really say that anyone looks English or anything else. Anybody can look anything."

"That's crazy," Luchita objected, thinking of Havana. Hastily she went on, "I lived in England for a while when I was young."

Mrs. Slade laughed merrily as she recalled her first impression of the girl standing in the patio.

"I went to art school there. That was when I decided to be an artist."

"Oh, you paint?" She sounded, but did not look, interested.

"I make drawings on paper. With pastels."

"Pastels are pretty," Mrs. Slade said in a colorless voice.

"If you want to see them I'll show them to you." At this point Luchita unconsciously applied a professional touch: a long look designed to convey an impression of sexy, childish innocence. Mrs. Slade gave no sign of having noticed it. She said, "Do bring them out. I'd love to see some."

Luchita sprang up, a little girl in her mother's new party dress, rustled across the room to a cabinet and drew out a portfolio.

The drawings were of uniform size. Carefully she laid them out in the middle of the floor in four rows, like playing cards. They were the work of a bright child that has absorbed certain formulas from looking at comic books. There were sunsets over the sea, heavily made-up film stars, and a few unidentifiable animals. Luchita stood up and remained looking down at them in an attitude of fond appreciation, her hands behind her back.

"What's that one?" Mrs. Slade asked in a toneless voice, pointing to an orange creature with many teeth, sprawled under a giant plant that looked like a cactus.

"Oh, that's a lion. I almost sold him one night at the Embassy Club. Then the man met a friend of his and they went away. He got too drunk, I guess."

"You sell them?" She tried to keep from sounding incredulous.

"Of course! That's why I make them. I'm trying to get the money to go back to Paris."

"But I don't understand," she began. "Aren't you living here? I mean, in this apartment?"

"Sometimes I stay," Luchita said vaguely. "Sometimes I go home."

"I see." Mrs. Slade was silent. "And you sell these in bars and places."

"A few weeks ago a man bought twenty. But it's not always like that."

"Twenty!"

110

"Vero thinks I should charge different prices. But I sell them for five dollars apiece."

"That seems reasonable," said Mrs. Slade guardedly. "They're awfully good. I hope you sell them all."

"Which ones do you like best?"

Here it comes, thought Mrs. Slade. "Oh, I like all of them," she said airily. "But I've never bought a picture in my life. I'd have no place to put it."

"Paris was fine. I used to make around eight thousand francs a day."

"You mean with your pictures?"

"I did them with chalk on the sidewalk. I always had a crowd."

"On the sidewalk!" she cried. "Have you done that here?"

"Vero says they don't allow it. But I could do it all right."

"You'd better not try."

Luchita knelt down and studied the drawings silently for a moment before gathering them up.

The girl's a mental case, she thought as she watched.

While Luchita was trying to get the portfolio back into the cabinet, the door opened and Señor Soto came in. "Sorry to be so long," he said smiling.

Mrs. Slade looked at him. "Where's Taylor?" And when he did not answer she said, "Where's Dr. Slade?"

He walked toward her with the same casual smile, as if he had not heard, and stood in front of her, regarding her quizzically from above. "He's all right. He wasn't feeling very well, so I had him lie down."

Mrs. Slade's eyes had opened wide. "Wasn't feeling well? What's the matter with him?"

Luchita had sunk down upon a hassock. She was convinced that once again Vero was lying, and it alarmed her because she could see no motive for it. He was patting Mrs. Slade on the shoulder. "If you want, I'll drive you out there right now, and we can all come back together. Or if not, I'll go out in a little while and get him. Either way."

"What's she going to do out at Los Hermanos?" demanded Luchita suddenly.

He did not take his eyes from Mrs. Slade's face. "Whichever you like."

Mrs. Slade sat for a moment, not moving; then she stood up. "May I have a vodka on the rocks?"

He moved one step backwards, his face showing dismay. "How about a sandwich and some salad? It's after nine."

She was protesting, "No, no, no," but he seemed not to hear her, and sent Luchita hurrying toward the kitchen.

"All I want is a drink," insisted Mrs. Slade, but he was already talking again. "You haven't seen this balcony out here. It's got a pool full of frogs."

She said nothing, and went with resentment; he was using the same tactics he had tried on her the previous day. As they passed through the doorway he seized her arm. Outside, they stood for an instant, looking up at the stars. He did not let go of the arm.

"This is more private," he was saying. "You don't get the wind. There's no view either, of course, except the trees."

Now he guided her toward the railing, and they leaned over, looking down at the street below, and out at the high pines not far away, black against the night-blue sky.

He sighed. "I thought we'd be going out on the town tonight. I wanted to show you and the Doctor a few

112

spots, two or three little places where the tourists never get." He paused. "Maybe we can make it for tomorrow. A good night's sleep tonight and he'll be back to normal. How old a man is he?"

"I believe he's sixty-seven," she said, resenting the question, and feeling somehow that she ought to have lied.

"Really. I'd have thought less than that by several years." He waited a moment. "Are you coming out there with me? The hacienda's worth seeing. Seventeenth century."

"I want a drink." Even in the dimness she knew he could see her looking straight at him.

"It's a magnificent old place," he went on, returning her stare, but decreasing the pressure of his fingers on her arm.

"A drink," she said again, slowly and clearly, her voice flickering with fury. She felt him let go of her.

"Yes. Of course." He turned and started inside.

You must calm down, she told herself. She moved nearer to the pool and parted the great smooth leaves of a liana that hung from the trellis above. A frog dived into the basin; the water made the sound of the word *blip*. She heard Señor Soto sliding open panels and clicking shut cabinet doors. She stood still.

When he came back out he was subdued, almost melancholy. "Well, here it is," he said, slowly handing her the glass. She imagined that his expression was wistful as he watched her drink. Soon Manuel arrived with a tray of sandwiches and brought her a plate.

"I'm glad to see you eating at last," he told her. "It'll be cold in the mountains."

She turned. "I'm not going. I'd rather stay here, if you don't mind."

"Of course, it's as you like." He did not try to conceal the displeasure in his voice.

"Look," she said. "I just don't feel like having to make an effort to control my nerves. Driving at night makes me nervous. You say he's not in danger and I take your word for it."

"Of course he's not in danger."

Luchita was standing in the doorway. "You need anything?" she asked.

"If you're not coming, I think I'll start out there now. I ought to be back here in about an hour."

"I'm sorry," she said, and then she began to flutter a bit. "We've made you so much trouble."

He turned at the doorway and looked back at her a second as if in surprise. Inside, he began to speak with Luchita. She heard their voices fading as they walked away into another room. It was about ten minutes before he went out.

19

Even on the small sheltered terrace it was too cool; she stepped inside. Luchita was sprawled on a pile of cushions, busy with cigarette papers. There was a feline-scented herbal smoke in the air.

"It's chilly outside," she announced.

Luchita looked up. "What's your name?" she said, as one small child to another.

Mrs. Slade stood still. "Why—"

"I mean, I heard the doctor call you Day. I wondered what it really was."

She was uncomfortable. "Well, it was—I mean it still is—" She laughed. "—Désirée. Dr. Slade never liked it, so he began calling me Day. You know. Anyway, I hate Désirée."

She felt that she had been clumsy in her explanation, for the girl did not appear to have understood. "You ought to make him call you Désirée," she said, looking straight ahead.

"He never would," Mrs. Slade said listlessly. He had told her that Day suited her; it was he who had to use the name. Suddenly she felt a physical dread, something pulling downward on each side of her body, and it seemed to her that the floor moved slightly. She stood very still, her heart beating fast.

"Do you have earthquakes here?" she asked presently, thinking of the emptiness beyond the balcony outside.

Luchita was more direct. "I didn't feel anything," she said, huddling with her knees up, wrapping her arms around her legs. "Did you?"

"I don't know." She stood in the middle of the room, irresolute, aware of an approaching wave of anguish. Luchita eyed her carefully. "You must be tired," she said. "Why don't you relax?"

Obediently she stretched out on the chinchilla spread. It might be possible to drive off the feeling of nausea. "I'm rather tense," she explained from where she lay.

"Relax," Luchita advised. Then she got up and turned down the lighting.

A while later Mrs. Slade spoke again. "I really don't feel very well. I don't think I'm going to be sick, though."

A gaseous blue light was beginning to glow somewhere behind her vision, and she had the impression

115

that there was a never-ending music, a music that was silent, yet present; it was like the wheezing, low notes of a harmonium. If she cleared her throat, she merely heard the sound of that over the music.

"You did too much today. You went too many places. You're not used to being up so high. It's awful. I hate it," Luchita was saying. She poured the chopped leaves into the machine and rolled out a new cigarette.

Presently Mrs. Slade sat up and stared across the room. "Malaria. Do you think I could have malaria? I really feel miserable. Terrible." The dread had seized her again, was twisting through her bowels.

"Malaria's nothing," Luchita said impassively. "You take a couple of pills."

Mrs. Slade lay down again. "It's so strong," she heard herself say as she shut her eyes. Then she fell back almost voluptuously into a world of undifferentiated flapping things where words were silent and colors became textures. There were blossomings and explosions. From where she had floated far down the coastline of her consciousness, she called out.

"I'm cold!" she cried.

Luchita came over to her quickly. She pressed her palm against Mrs. Slade's forehead.

"You haven't got malaria," she told her. Then she tossed another light fur spread over her. In her mind was the idea that if she got too close to Mrs. Slade she might carry the disease to Pepito.

"You ought to have a doctor," she said uncertainly. "Only you'll have to wait until Vero comes back. He knows the name of a doctor." Then she began to laugh. "I'm crazy! Your husband. He's your doctor!"

Mrs. Slade heard her words, but she heard each one separately; each was a point of departure for a new idea, something completely different. A vast novel was unfolding; she recognized the backdrop as a sinister distortion of the actual landscape outside the apartment. The countryside was peopled, but she could not see the faces. Now and then, with the regularity of a nerve aching, the conviction swept over her that the faces belonged to an unknown monstrous race. She was being propelled toward a time when they would no longer be hidden.

She moaned a little. Luchita looked up, apprehensive. "I'll put on some music," she said. Vero had told her, "Please don't monkey with the tape recorder or the phonograph. I've got them both set up the way I want." She flicked the tape recorder on anyway: African drumming, incisive, perfect in rhythm, endlessly repetitive. Then she went back to her work. The precise patterns played on, minute after minute. He had said another thing that struck her as peculiar: "If I'm not back by midnight, have Mrs. Slade stay here. Put her in your old room." She hoped he would come early. It was bad enough that she herself should not be allowed to have the room, without being obliged to offer it to a stranger.

The landscape was flaking off, crumbling. Day sat erect again, staring around the room. Luchita saw the movement and looked up.

"Can I get you something? Some hot tea? Some cold Coke?"

Mrs. Slade saw the room becoming gelatinous; she watched the opposite wall quiver and shimmer like the top of an aspic. "Cold Coke," she repeated thickly, without inflection. "Cold Coke."

A moment later, when Luchita returned from the kitchen, she was lying out flat. She spoke to her, but there was no reply. Luchita set the glass down. "It's there on the table when you want it," she told her. Then it occurred to her that if Mrs. Slade were really ill, it would be wiser to put her to bed now, before she fell asleep or became delirious.

She finally got her to her feet, but she would not walk. "I can't be pushed any further!" she cried desperately, and looked at Luchita, her eyes starting out of her head, as if she were seeing her for the first time. "Where's my husband?"

She's acting, thought Luchita, seeing the distraught, haunted expression on her face. She took her arm, said, "We have to go out through the patio," and led her on a crooked course in that direction. When they got to the bedroom the long silk curtains were blowing inward with the breeze. "The bathroom's here." Luchita reached her arm through a dark doorway and switched on a light. Out of the corner of her eye she saw Mrs. Slade about to sink down onto the bed. "No, no!" she cried, running back to stop her. "Sit here." She eased her into a chair and pressed a wall button fiercely. While she waited for the maid she took the fur spread off the bed, turned the sheets back and patted the pillows. There was a knock at the door; she opened it and spoke in a low voice with Paloma for a moment. Then she turned back to Mrs. Slade, who sat slumped in the chair wringing her hands. "Paloma's going to help you. Just relax and go to sleep."

Since Mrs. Slade did not appear to have heard her, Luchita went out and shut the door.

Paloma eyed the foreign lady mistrustfully; she had seen enough gringas to decide straightway that this one was drunk. She forced her up out of the chair and pulled off her dress and slip. Then she got a challis dressing gown from the closet. The wind was still blowing in through the doors that gave on to the balcony, and the curtains rippled fitfully into the room. The lady was shivering; she continued to tremble and shake uncontrollably as she got into the bed with the bathrobe belt finally tied around her waist. Paloma watched her for a moment, and came to a different conclusion: the lady took drugs. She had seen films in which addicts were shown behaving very much as she was behaving now. And she continued to stare downward, an expression of disgust spreading over her face as she watched. Mrs. Slade's palsied hands clawed frantically at the sheet; she was trying to cover herself. Paloma only looked. She did not lean over to help her. The gringa was not a person. That's what they come to, she told herself.

The smooth linen sheets were painfully cold; wherever they touched her, they hurt—on the high peaks where the snow glistened and in the valleys where the glaciers creaked. It was all painful, the pain of cold like the aching of an inmost nerve.

Even while she was balancing at the edge of the abyss, she found herself wondering that it was possible to be in so decentralized a state and yet be aware, not only of everything inside and outside herself, but also of the fact that the disintegration was still in process.

There was, of course, no bottom to the abyss, once she had been drawn into it. It was merely a further stage of decomposition, the inability to respond to the law of gravity. The fall was slow, almost luxurious. When it gathered speed and she grew dizzy, she opened her eyes. A strange woman stood over her; she had a face of luminous white wax. Her eyes were staring down at the bed with an expression of hatred. She screamed once

119

and sat up, stretched out her arm to drive away the demon. It turned swiftly and clicked off all the lights. Then it went out of the room and shut the door.

The distant sound of the wind blowing through the pines was a little like the roar of the sea; it rose up from below now and then and came through the doors into the room.

Inside, in the dark vault of her consciousness, there was an endless entry into Hell, where cities toppled and crashed upon her, and she died each time slowly, imprisoned at the bottom of the wreckage. And on the fiery horizon still more cities towered, postponing their imminent collapse until she should be within reach.

20

THERE IS A COLD wind blowing along the floor; it is that way in all the rooms so far. It comes from the patio. The doors are shut but it blows under them. He can feel it on his ankles. He is walking without shoes, wearing a bathrobe, but he is not thinking about that. Thus far he has found a door from each room into the next, so that he has not had to go out into the patio. There are dim lights out there among the bushes. The rooms are in darkness. That is good, because it is safer in the dark, even though he bumps into things sometimes as he feels his way along.

He listens and hears frogs singing, but they sound far away. The rooms smell old; they have that inner stillness found only in ancient houses. As he passes an open door into the patio, he looks out for an instant and sees stone pillars and arches. He moves ahead, but with such caution that even when he comes suddenly upon a piece of furniture, he makes no sound as he touches it.

He does not know where he is trying to go; he only wants to get as far as possible from the bed. The dream he has left there was so terrible he cannot remember it. But this could still be part of the dream, he thinks, bristling with fear, this unchanging silent house with the men somewhere in it waiting to catch him. In a dream, what does it matter? Strike out, smash the furniture, yell. Let them come rushing through the rooms.

He holds his breath, listens again. Frogs. A dog yaps in the distance. Now he knows that he wants to get out of the house. When he starts to move again he is less cautious, and comes up short against a chair. To keep as far as he can from the patio, he makes his way toward the opposite wall. On the far side of one of the rooms he may find a door, and the door could open onto the garden. When his outstretched hand touches a curtain, his fingers follow the cloth to its end; he pulls the curtain back a bit and steps behind its folds. The window is high and has iron grillwork over it. But the sight of the stars excites him. They're still there, he thinks. At the same instant a twinge of fear makes him peer around, back into the room. He had forgotten fear for a while; he had merely been on his way. He remembers: it began as a nightmare. Now it is beginning to turn back into one. He waits for the signs of transformation, and because there is no change in the silence and darkness of the room, he suddenly becomes aware that neither the silence nor the darkness is complete. There is the sound of leaves being moved by a faint breeze in the patio; the basic glow of the stars coming in through a door, a window, can sometimes help to determine the size and even the shape of a desk or chair. At this moment he is convinced that he is awake, that the soles of his bare feet actually are touching the soft rugs and icy tiles; they are surfaces that supply varying sensations. But what is the world? he thinks. How many more rooms are there in it?

The stucco wall along which he has been feeling his way ends in a smooth wooden pillar. A little more light comes from the patio into the next room, and he hears a cricket outside. A variation in the quality of the acoustics, and he glances upward. This room is much higher than the others; he imagines he sees a balcony up there in the dark at the far end.

The big room proves to have no door leading into a further room. His eyes follow the curve of an archway that gives onto the patio. As he approaches it, the sweet nocturnal smell of plant life comes in, on an eddy of breeze, and the odor disturbs him. To escape its impact he makes himself take a step forward through the archway and peer outside. A small lantern hangs some distance back in the bushes beyond the arcade, masked by moving leaves. To the left is a wide staircase leading upward. There is still no sound but the frogs calling in chorus from a distance and the drier chirp of a few crickets in the patio. Quickly he walks across that corner of the cloistered passage and starts to climb. The steps are made of smooth stone, and they slant slightly toward the center, where the tread of feet has worn them down.

Now he hears a voice. It seems to be calling from one room to another, far at the other end of the house. "Yes," it says. Then he can hear nothing. He continues silently. Up here the patio looks the same; the arched balcony stretches out to the left and straight ahead. The stars are more in evidence: no branches hide them.

He goes swiftly to the nearest open door and enters. In the patio he would be visible. He believes that he is likely to find a way out of the house in one of these rooms up here. This floor is much more difficult. The rooms are only partially furnished, and there are crates and piles of boxes along the walls. The first two rooms are filled with the heavy odor of ancient dust. The third makes him stop short: it smells lived in. He moves ahead uncertainly. All at once there is an object in front of him, very near to his right eye. He draws back and looks up. It is a piece of sculpture, towering dimly above him. He feels he is going to lose his balance and takes a step sideways, bending exaggeratedly to avoid the statue. His arm stretches out ahead of him and his hand strikes something cold and very smooth, and during that instant there is a loud sound in the room.

In the following silence he listens first and hears nothing. He has not even asked himself what has happened, what has caused the sound. He listens, still hears nothing. While he is listening, he is growing used to his surroundings: he is standing in front of a grand piano, his head bent, looking downward. But now he hears something. It is at first as much felt under his feet as heard, like a bump. Then in the patio a slight stirring of sound is added to the call of the crickets and the air moving the leaves.

They are coming up the stairs, indifferent to the noise their shoes are making on the steps. He stands there and waits. Without warning, the room is bursting with light, as from a great altitude he gazes down upon the precise black-and-white landscape of the keyboard.

They are being very polite, joking carefully with him as they gently guide him through the door and across the covered passage to the stairway. One of them keeps tell-

123

ing him that he has a fever and ought to be in bed. He replies that it is not true, but that he was expecting them to come in any case. They seem a little in awe of him, and he feels that this respect is predicated upon his complete obedience; at the first sign of a divergency of opinion or behavior on his part their attitude will change. He has always known the world is like this. There is no way of escaping. They come and get you and quietly lead you away. As they go down the stone steps they are telling him that he is risking pneumonia, that he must understand he is ill, that he must stay in bed.

Now they are back down in the other half of the world. He feels that he knows it intimately: the lantern behind the leaves as they go along under the arches, the crickets' song, the open doors into the dark rooms, and the doors that are shut, where the wind blows underneath.

When they are in his room and he sees the bed, he looks up at them, waiting to be told to get in. One of them announces he is going to make him some hot tea, that he may have caught a chill. He says that if it were not for the fever he would give him brandy instead.

"Fever?" he repeats thickly, climbing into the bed. "Fever?" He turns his head to one side, shuts his eyes, and lies still. In one respect they are right, the two young strangers: he feels very ill.

Much later, as someone comes in, he opens his eyes. The only light is behind a high screen; the bed is in shadow. One of the young men is walking toward him carrying a cup and saucer. He stares up from the pillows; it does not surprise him to see that his captor's face is painted in stripes of blue and black. Around the snout the stripes run together in a more delicate design; this part of the face is faintly incandescent. He thinks he has motioned to him to put the cup on the table. He tells himself that he expected it, but the striped mask disturbs him and he does not want any contact with its owner.

He has made no signal at all; he has not moved. The creature forces him to sit up and drink the tea, so hot that it burns his lips. It seems a long time before he has drunk it and is allowed to lie down. He has not glanced at the face again. The young man walks away. As he is leaving the room he stands in the doorway an instant and tells him that Mr. Soto will soon be there. He says it with an air of promising something pleasant, as if he too is looking forward to the arrival.

When he lies alone in the darkened room once more, the absurd idea comes into his head that these people are invaders from outer space. No one ever had such a face, he is certain; he looked directly at it and saw the miniature designs around the muzzle.

The visitor, when he comes, proves to be another like the first two, only larger and more officious; he is clearly their commander. This one has no stripes on his face. On the contrary, it would seem that no effort had been spared to make him as realistic as possible. He is a facsimile made with the most meticulous regard for detail; he is a perfect imitation of a man. And now that the lights have been turned on, he sees that the other one no longer bears the stripes on his snout. They burned away, he thinks.

The chief comes toward the bed, his hands in his pockets. "How you feeling now, Doctor? A little better?" He cocks his head to one side.

"I'm all right."

"The pills helped." The chief says this as a question, with a note of faint astonishment.

He only grunts, and moves a little in the bed, aware

that the chief has come closer and is standing over him, moving objects on the table by his pillow.

"May have brought it down," he hears him say, and he feels the end of a thermometer being pushed against his lip.

Yes, he is sick, he thinks, but the synthetic man has no idea of what is the matter with him; he is playing the doctor tonight. He rolls the thermometer under his tongue and looks up at him distrustfully. Later the chief pulls it out of his mouth and holds it under the lamp on the table to read it; he turns his head toward the wall and keeps his eyes shut while this is going on.

"Very good," the chief says after a moment. "Down to a hundred and three point two."

He makes a momentous decision—that of forcing himself to go to the trouble of sitting up. The chief looks at him in surprise as he sees him begin to struggle upward.

"May I see it?" he hears himself say. The chief quickly hands him the thermometer, saying, "You ought not to be making any effort."

"I can read a thermometer," he replies tonelessly. It takes him a long time; he is trying to focus on the painted notches and catch the magnified gleam of the mercury behind the curve of the glass. He holds it very close to his eyes. The silver band inside is there, but then he loses it, and the effort to regain it is more than he can make. He grunts and hands it back, certain, as he pushes his head into the pillows, that there is no fever. He cries out, "Why don't you just try leaving me alone?"

The chief laughs indulgently. "You've got to eat. It's essential to keep something inside you."

When he has drunk the consommé and eaten the sandwich he lies down with his head facing away from the lamp. A moment later someone comes quietly in and switches off all the lights.

There is a mistake about the time. He is in a house, caught in the body of a man who is being kept in bed. People come and bother him, go away. Doors are opened and shut. It is daytime; it is night. Sometimes he is impaled on the wind as he rushes through space. There are long periods when he is imprisoned in a muddy submarine world, aware of the room beyond the bed, knowing that time is creeping past, but able only to lie there without motion, clinging mollusk-like to the underside of consciousness until someone comes and touches him, and once again changes everything.

21

THERE CAME a moment when she found herself knowing it was daytime rather than night, and when she was aware of one hour following upon another. She was in the open air, lying in bed on a balcony. Birds chirped from the railing; the wind smelled of gardenias and pine trees. But this is real, she thought with a shock, and in the desperate hope of finding it possible to remain with the reality she decided to make no effort, merely to watch and see what would happen.

Several times that morning the nurse brought her food and cold drinks. It was logical to suppose there must be someone else nearby, but she had no memory of anyone but the nurse. Often she suspected her of not being a nurse at all; the woman's ill-humor was more like that of a sullen menial. She felt that for her to have been left in the hands of such a person was a serious oversight on someone's part, and she intended to complain about it when the right time came. She tried not to let herself dislike the nurse too much: she suspected the other would sense it and retaliate in some indirect manner. Always the woman came in a hurry, tapping along the tiles on her little high heels, did what had to be done on the balcony with visible distaste and a great deal of noise, and then went away again without even looking at her. When she was gone and the balcony was quiet once more, she would lie in a state of sheer happiness, grateful for having been returned to the world outside. Convalescence, she told herself comfortably, without troubling to wonder from what.

At sunset she heard hushed voices in the room off the balcony. She opened her eyes and stared ahead of her, listening, thinking she recognized one of the voices. "Doctor," she cried feebly. The murmur stopped; there was silence. For a while she waited, expecting the conversation to start up once more, and when it did not, trying to hear at least the sound of retreating footsteps. After a while she called out again, "Nurse!" The word seemed to have come up out of a distant valley; it was hard to believe that it was she who had uttered it. Still there was no sound from the room. She waited a long time; no one came, and there were no more voices. The birds had gone and it was almost dark. Feeling hurt and resentful, she drifted off into sleep.

A floor lamp had been put beside the bed. The light was shining into her face, and a man stood there looking down at her. She assumed he was the doctor. Behind him stood another man, much younger; this one she recognized, without connecting him with any specific place or particular period of her life.

She tried to smile at the doctor, but she was not sure whether the muscles of her face had moved or not. "I'm better," she said.

The doctor, without ceasing to look at her, said something to the other in Spanish. Then he bent over and lifted her hand to his lips, letting it drop gently back onto the coverlet. He straightened, turned, and walked inside, followed by the younger man. She wanted to call after them; instead, she lay still under the blinding light, listening to their voices recede as they went through the rooms, finally hearing them die out entirely.

Some time later there were approaching footsteps. The young man came out onto the balcony, smiling, his hands in his pockets. "Sorry to leave that light in your eyes," he said, and turned it off. The balcony was half in light, half in shadow.

"You're a lot better, aren't you?" It was a statement which he expected her to confirm, but she said nothing. "Are you really out of the tunnel now?"

Still she did not answer; she imagined herself walking in a tunnel and seeing the opening ahead. At first the mouth of the tunnel was fairly near, but then it grew smaller and smaller. She opened her eyes quickly. He was looking at her with undisguised interest.

"This is the first day," she said, and wondered if he understood what she meant. There she lay at the bottom of her soft world while he talked of symptoms, treatment and reactions, idly asking herself now and then what his function was in the hospital. It was all one unchanging scene; he ended it rather abruptly, she thought, by saying "Good night" and walking away. At some point the nurse must have come, for when she awoke later the balcony was in darkness, and she could see the stars in the sky beyond the railing.

The next day she was more at home inside herself. When the young man came she said to him, "I'm out of the tunnel."

"I can see that." He was wearing a red and gray striped shirt and a pair of shorts. She stared with mild astonishment at his bare legs.

"You're not the doctor, are you?"

He smiled condescendingly. "You saw the doctor yesterday. You've finished with him. He's seeing Dr. Slade today. Also for the last time. You're both out of your respective tunnels."

He went on talking, but for a moment she did not hear what he was saying. She had been lying here all this time, and not once had the thought of Taylor crossed her mind. If he'd asked me was I married, I'd have said no, she marveled. After a while the meaning of his words came to her, and she interrupted him, crying, "Is Dr. Slade ill?"

"He's fine. He's fine." The young man patted her hand. "You've both been sick, and you're both well." He looked carefully at her.

She did not reply. If she had known who the young man was, in what capacity he served on the staff, she reflected, it would have been easier for her to talk with him. There were the complaints she wanted to make about the service and the nurse they had assigned to her. But she had a feeling that the young man had the answers to all possible questions written out and hidden away for safekeeping, and that under no circumstances would she ever get from him more than a small part of the truth. With this in mind, it seemed scarcely worth while to ask; nevertheless she did. "Where is he? Where is Taylor?"

"Right there at Los Hermanos where he's been the whole time." If he had said, "Still undergoing gravitational therapy on Venus," she would have understood just as much. But she answered, "I see," as though she now had a clear picture of a life being led in a place called The Brothers, and as though it were to be expected that her husband should be leading that life. Even as he said the words, however, her mind was brushed by the shadow of another question she could not even formulate. An intensity in the young man's eyes had belied the simulated casualness of his reply.

Since she said no more, he ceased staring at her and lit a cigarette. "I think you can plan on seeing him tomorrow night," he told her presently. "Would you like some music?"

"I don't think so. Not particularly."

It was as though the world no longer contained anything certain. There were only unstable elements; everything had been cut free, was floating. Her head was clear; she was aware of being able to follow and assess her thoughts. Yet without finding it possible to name it specifically, she was convinced that something in the situation was amiss, something outside and beyond her own lassitude. As she grew stronger, she reflected, it was likely that she would be less conscious of it, and precisely for that reason she made a mental note to remind herself of it the next day.

He talked for a while. She pretended to be drifting off now and then into sleep. At length he left her.

She swung her legs over the side of the bed and took a few tentative steps, barefoot, on the cold tiles. Feeling surprisingly full of energy, she began to walk up and

131

down alongside the railing, looking out at the patterns made by the occasional street lights of some remote suburb across the valley.

At the far end of the balcony there was a small lavatory; a mirror hung above the washbasin. In its reflection she searched for signs of illness or fatigue and was mildly astonished to find none. But then a whole series of unanswerable questions flooded her mind simultaneously. Where was her handbag? Where had they put her clothes? What hospital was it? In the mirror she saw her eyes open a little wider as she was seized by the realization that she could remember nothing of arriving, whether she thought of the hospital or of the city whose lights she had seen a moment ago.

She looked down into the washbasin, bent over, and began to splash cold water into her face. She understood that she had not yet fully recovered; probably it had been unwise of her to get up and walk even this much. At all events, and she said this to herself with great firmness, it was important not to be afraid. She dried her face pleasurably with a large bath towel; the best thing would be to get back into bed and sleep.

When she awoke at dawn the problem was there with her, an invisible, total curtain between her and everything outside. The frail strand of cockcrow that came over the still air was filtered through the curtain, and thus reached her devoid of meaning. She knew that somewhere roosters were crowing, but because she could not remember how she had got to this high balcony in a town she did not know, the roosters' very existence was unacceptable. She felt her heart begin to beat very hard, like something wholly apart from her. Coughing nervously, she thought of adrenalin, the product of fear. It was imperative to hold out until Taylor came. She sat up

132

and looked out at the large moon still casually giving light, like a street lamp left on after day has come. The pointed black tips of some pine trees not far away showed above the railing. There was only the unnecessary moon to look at, and as she looked, life began to move again, because all at once she had remembered. The fact that an hour or so later she discovered a few empty spots in the landscape of the past did not bother her greatly; she felt that she had found the important material.

The nurse brought her a fine breakfast. She ate it all and lay quietly watching the sparrows arrive and shower drops of water from the birdbath. It was on the ship where the story began to blur, where details became uncertain. She could not recapture the image of their cabin; had it been port or starboard? And in the dining room. She thought she recalled a meal when she had been eating rice, sitting across from Taylor, but had it been on the ship?

When she saw the young man arriving at half-past ten, the unwelcome idea came to her that he might be a supervising psychiatrist: he was so cocksure, so clearly in command.

"Paloma says you're back into yourself, as she put it," he told her, beaming with pleasure. "Yes. You look about ready to set forth."

"Set forth?"

"Yes." He smiled harder and, leaning over, rested his hands on the knobs of the footboard. "For the country."

"I don't know what you're talking about!" she cried excitedly. "The country? What for? Didn't you tell me Dr. Slade would be here tonight?"

He shook his head, still smiling. "You misunderstood. Not here. At San Felipe."

She sat very stiff and severe, certain that an edge of anger must show in her voice. "Look!" she said. "I'm not the kind that takes orders. My mechanism doesn't work. There's just no reaction." She waited a moment, and then, since he did not answer, she went on. "Why can't my husband come here and see me? Is it forbidden, or what?"

The young man straightened and viewed her with surprise.

"Come on," she urged him. "I'm very dense, I know, but is there any reason why Dr. Slade can't visit me here at the hospital?"

"Hospital! You don't recognize the apartment?"

Without ceasing to look at her, he lowered himself slowly into a chair. After a moment he went on calmly, "It can come after the fever. It's nothing. It goes away." He leaned forward. "You had an extremely high fever for a while, in case you don't know."

"I don't want to hear about it." Apartment, she was thinking.

He laughed. "Better not to."

The nurse came clacking onto the balcony, saw the young man, and stood still. Then she bowed respectfully toward the bed and said, "*Muy buenos días, señora.*"

"I'm going to leave you with Paloma." He started away, then paused in the doorway to say, "Your things are in here, in this room. I think you'll find everything. When you're dressed, why don't you call Luchita on the phone? Push number four. I'll be back here for lunch." He chuckled. "And you really thought this was a hospital!"

The room was large and pleasantly cool. All the valises, hers and Taylor's, stood in a corner. She went into the bathroom and turned on the hot water. The tub was a good place for lying back and thinking. Her outburst had been regrettable, but he had taken it very well. She smiled at her toes, seeing them sticking out above the water level. It was still an embarrassing situation, to be the house guest of people whose name she did not even know.

When she went back into the bedroom Paloma was waiting for her to unlock her bags. Finally she was dressed, and although she had no desire to meet her hostess, she took up the telephone and pressed the number four button. Fortunately it was the young man who answered; a minute later he was at the door, and together they walked through a patio and several rooms, out onto a spacious terrace. I've probably seen all this before, she told herself; it even seemed to her that she recalled certain things, but it was more as though she had read about them or seen them in a film.

They stood talking in the shade by a pool where some lianas hung; still he had given her no clue. Suddenly she saw the city gleaming in the haze far below, and as she became aware of the great height, she took a few steps back toward the wall of the building.

"You remember this terrace?" he inquired.

"I can't even tell you. That means I don't, I suppose."

"We came out here. And we talked about a building. The building at the end of the dock. How it seemed to collapse, you remember, when you fell?"

As he spoke, she lowered her head a little and passed her hand over her eyes. She had a static image, in which she and Taylor were in a huge dusty windowless tin-covered shed—an inferno of heat and noise. They were both sick, and being sick they were afraid. Remembering it now was like skirting the black flames of a noonday nightmare. Taylor had just remarked that if only he could get to the door and breathe some fresh air he would be all right. And then he had fallen, and she must have run ahead to the door to look for help. Now she saw what was like a color photo in an advertisement: a pair of handsome young people attractively dressed in beach clothes standing by a sports car under a coconut palm. The world had suddenly turned sideways like a plane banking, and as she fell she had seen a frame building at the end of the next pier cave in as if a giant foot had kicked it.

"The sun's hot," she said. "Could we go in?"

"You did tell me about how the building seemed to buckle and collapse?"

"Yes," she said in a faint voice, walking on toward the door. "In Puerto Farol. We can never thank you for all you've done."

"You were a sick couple, that I'll say."

When they were inside she sat on a pile of cushions and shielded her eyes. "The sun makes me dizzy," she confided. She remembered the fur and the glass and the tall plants, the strange child with her pictures spread out on the floor, the moment when she had begun to be cold, and then the slow journey down into the cloaca of horror that had been the disease. She was silent.

"I'm going to fix you a drink," he said.

When the girl came in and he cried, "Ah, Luchita!" it was the same child who had shown the drawings, the same child who had stood glistening in the picture postcard of the car under the palms.

"Hello," she said. "Are you all right now?"

"Yes. I'm fine."

He spoke from the other side of the room. "Everybody ought to be at San Felipe by seven at the latest. Luchita can drive you down in the station wagon."

"I want a bottle of Seven-Up," Luchita announced.

"You'll have to get it from the kitchen," he told her.

Mrs. Slade and her host were alone for a moment. "What does she call you?" she asked him. "Vero?"

"Evolved from Grover through Grovero. Sort of a joke, like *pocho* talk in reverse." He eyed her sharply. "I thought it would be good if you and Dr. Slade saw something of the country before you left. Some of the mountains, some of the jungle. It's a beautiful drive down to San Felipe." He described a series of hairpin turns with his forefinger. "If you like scenery."

"I do. I never get tired of it."

Luchita had come back into the room carrying a tall glass; ice cubes clinked daintily against its sides. "It's *tierra caliente*," she said, looking meaningfully at Mrs. Slade, and he glanced her way with annoyance.

"Is it very hot there?" Mrs. Slade wanted to know.

Luchita had caught his warning. "Not too bad," she said.

"I somehow don't think it would be good to stay too long in a place where it was very hot, do you?"

"It isn't hot," he told her. "That wasn't what Luchita meant. *Tierra caliente* isn't necessarily hot. She just doesn't like *tierra caliente*. The ranch isn't in the selva. It's in the open, just above where the selva begins."

The drink was helping. After a moment she said, "All I can tell you is that I'm overcome by so much attention. You have to come all the way here to find out what real hospitality is."

It would be better not to show any hesitation in accepting; then when she and Taylor got together they could make their plans. Lunch was an elaborate curry; the big table was entirely covered with side dishes.

When they had finished coffee, she felt a good deal livelier.

"About the luggage, you want to take everything, I imagine," he told her. "You may want to go on to whereever you're going from there."

He helped the doorman pack the car, and waved as Luchita swung the station wagon around and started down the mountainside. In the city, after they had left the business district, Luchita got a traffic ticket for being on the left of the white line in the center of the street. "Vero's going to be mean when I tell him," Luchita sighed.

"You have to pick the right moment."

Steering her way slowly between oxcarts and crowds of barefoot pedestrians, Luchita laughed derisively. Soon they were in the country.

22

THERE WAS THE SKY, and then trees went past, first nearby, overhead, with huge shining green leaves. The sky came again, and more trees far away on the side of a stony hill, gray, leafless, spiked, hundreds of them, while more of the hill came into view. The train jerked as it went along, making his head rock from side to side. The air that blew in through the window above his head was foul with coal gas. Now and then a tiny cinder pellet hit his face. He was about to move his hand up to cover his forehead, but at the same instant his mind began to move. His eyes shut and he lay still. He would wait until he knew more before venturing out of his hiding place. The idea came to him that perhaps it would be better to go all the way back in; if he were surprised out there he would be helpless. Let him begin to think too much, and they would sense it. He wanted to spy on them from the safety of the dark.

The next time he came back, his eyes were open again, and he saw the sky and trees the same as before. Then he glanced once down along his body and shut his eyes. He was intact, and he wore his gray slacks and had sandals on his feet. His heart was beating too fast and hard, but inside his mind there was calm.

He slept a little, aware betweentimes of the train running on and on, roaring over trestles, the sound of its wheels echoing against hillsides.

He opened his eyes and looked across the compartment. Only one man was sitting there, young, carefully dressed, heavily tanned by the sun. Yes, he thought. I know him. It was surprising that there should be only this one; he had been sure there were several. Then it occurred to him that the young man was speaking to him, and that he in turn was expected to say something. He pushed himself up a bit and shook his head dubiously. The sensation of helplessness was real now; it was like early morning in a strange hotel room when for a moment the waker has no idea of where he is. But that nowhereness is always dispelled after a few instants of effort, and this was still going on.

He peered more closely at the young man. He looked like a film star, and he spoke in the almost convincing manner of a character in a film, his face constantly

139

changing a little in its expression as it accompanied his sentences. It was important to know what he was talking about.

"I don't know," he said dubiously; now he too was a character in the same film. He studied the gray eyes behind the handsome mobile face.

The young man smiled reassuringly. There was a large pigskin valise in the rack over his head; a raincoat lay folded on top of it.

They were together on a train. He was making a trip with this young man whose name escaped him, and he was getting old. Old. That was the only explanation. But it seemed likely that if the other talked enough, he would remember. Some word would come out which would make the connection and bring him entirely awake.

The young man looked at his watch. "The girls ought to be at Escobar around about now. There's a sort of inn there where they'll probably stop for something."

What he was saying conveyed no message. "You'll have to excuse me," he said, endeavoring to sit up a bit straighter. "I'm a little muzzy. How long have I been asleep?"

"I don't know. A while."

They rushed into the dark of a tunnel and were out again into the open, the train straining around a long curve. "What were you saying a few minutes ago?" he said.

The young man laughed shortly. "Whatever it was, it was just an opening gambit. I didn't want to startle you."

"Startle me?"

"You see, I was sure you'd make sense one of these times when you came around, and finally you did."

For some reason he felt a surge of anger. "Why don't

you say whatever it is you're trying to say? Haven't I been making sense?"

The other leaned forward on the seat and looked at him intently. "You're fine now. But you weren't so hot a few days ago. You know, it's tricky where the brain's involved. You might easily have waked up just now without any idea of who the hell you were."

The word "brain" carried dark echoes with it. "I know who I am," he said grimly, shutting his eyes. But it was true: he was still muzzy. He occupied a small center of unknown territory, and on all sides there was wilderness. And that was exactly what the young man had meant: amnesia.

"What was it? What did I manage to pick up?"

The young man sat back. "There's a lot of it around," he said. "They don't really know much about how it works. A man named Newbold isolated the virus a few years ago. It's called after him. Hits like lightning and goes away just as fast, without doing any visible harm. Except, as I say, sometimes there's this temporary memory loss."

"Hmmm." He let his eyes follow the pattern in the lace on the armrest. It was like a first-class compartment on a European train. This disturbed him: he did not want to be in Europe.

"How temporary is it?" he finally said. "I ask because I've got it. I'm *lost!*" He shook his head slowly.

"No, you're not. Look. You remember landing in Puerto Farol with Day?"

The names were enough; the contact was made. Once more he shut his eyes. As the darkness inside was banished, he recalled the sea-smell of the town, green and steaming after rain. The train swerved, whistled, clattered along the edge of a cliff. "Where is she?" he said.

"On the highway down there somewhere, behind those nearest mountains, in a white station wagon." The young man thrust his arm out the window and pointed.

He lay back for a bit, having decided against asking all the other questions. If he waited until he was clearer-headed, perhaps he would not have to ask them at all.

"We came in this contraption because I wanted you to be able to lie out flat. Anyway, Los Hermanos is on the line to San Felipe. It's the easiest way."

He grunted a reply and realized that he was half asleep once again. Then the young man said no more; the sounds and movements of the train took over.

He felt his shoulder being prodded; the rasping sound of brakes filled the coach. He sat up and put his feet on the floor. The train was winding through a narrow gorge with sheer rock walls on either side. "Is this it?" he asked, and the other nodded. The gorge widened, the train kept braking, and he saw a small dust-colored town ahead.

"I take it the bags are all in the car," he said to the young man.

"That's right. Everything."

The train stopped and they stood up. Taking his suitcase and raincoat, the young man pushed him ahead into the corridor. "You go ahead and I'll be right behind."

"This is really something," he muttered, shuffling along with difficulty. "Come on a vacation and wind up like this. . . ."

"You're doing fine. Just keep going."

They rode in a truck, down into warmer land, the three of them: the mestizo driver, the young man and he. The countryside was covered with flat-topped, leafless thorn trees. Ahead the orange sky flared, then faded, and the spiny landscape went ghost-gray.

"Day's been down with it too, you know," the young

142

man said suddenly, adding, "You'd never believe it, though. I swear, she looks better now than she did before. I didn't know whether to tell you or let her tell you."

"Hell, don't keep any secrets from me. She's all right?"

"Blossoming. I took care of a case of Newbold's right here at the ranch last year. This friend of mine was really sick. But it was incredible! He was up and running around five days later, exactly as if nothing had happened. When I say sick, I mean I thought he wasn't going to pull through. Photism and convulsions and all the trimmings."

"Good God!"

The truck stopped and they got out. In the near-dark he could see only a long windowless wall. The air, warm and dry, was sweet with the smell of woodsmoke. Half a dozen servants ran up, each carrying a flashlight. There were greetings and handshakings; these continued as they went into the house and more servants appeared.

"If you'll just come through here," the young man said. "I'm putting you two in this wing by yourselves. You'll have absolute privacy. It's a pretty big house. Used to be a monastery, you know." He pointed to the beamed ceiling. A barefoot Indian girl carrying a thermos bottle appeared through a doorway ahead of them; she smiled shyly as they passed her.

"You'd probably like to eat something light, right in your room, and go to bed."

"You're right," he said with feeling.

The young man knocked on the door through which the maid had just come, and Day opened it.

THREE

23

DR. SLADE HAD FINISHED his breakfast. The table was set under a khaki-colored parasol in the small patio off the bedroom. He turned his chair around so he could look across the garden. "They've done everything they could for us," he said.

"They've been marvelous, of course. I often wonder what we must have looked like, staggering out of that customs office." Being with Taylor had brought her all the way back into the world; she sat and enjoyed the powerful early morning sunlight and the country smells. "No! I only meant—you don't want to stay here *very* long, do you? They couldn't be sweeter and more generous." She hesitated and took a sip of coffee. "But what have we got in common?"

This of course was the position he had originally taken with regard to his hosts, but at the moment he was in an expansive mood. He stretched back in his chair and yawned. "You're talking too soon, Day. You can't tell. You may love it here."

"You keep inferring there's something here I don't like. I'm divinely happy. I wouldn't want to be anywhere else. But from something you said, I got the impression you felt like staying for quite a while, and I'm just trying to find out how long."

"Since we're here, why don't we just enjoy ourselves? Whenever you want, we can leave."

She sighed. He was not in the habit of being relaxed and casual when it was a question of travel plans. It could be a sign of fatigue. At his age, she reflected, and considering the virulence of the disease, he was fortunate to have rallied this quickly.

"I suppose you're right," she said, feeling a sudden surge of protectiveness toward him. It seemed likely that he needed a thorough rest, and this was the opportunity. She stretched out her feet in front of her and looked at her sandals. "We'll save money, too," she added archly.

He grunted. "It's usually about the same as a hotel by the time you get out, as far as that goes." Her abrupt gesture of agreement had not escaped him; however, he was wary of its motive, and waited.

Late in the afternoon, when the shadows were oblique, they set forth on a walking tour of inspection under the guidance of Señor Soto. Luchita was sullen and silent, and made a point of looking at the sky or the ground beneath her feet each time they stopped to admire a view or examine a plant. She wore a torn shirt, a pair of exaggeratedly dirty Levis, and from what Day could see, nothing else. At one point they came out onto a point of tableland overlooking the river valley and the forest below. "It's dry jungle," said their host. "You can see it's really only a strip that follows the river. We've got about ten thousand acres of good grazing land on the other side over there. Down below here there's a little coffee. Not much, yet. It costs more than it brings in at this point."

Day glanced around for Luchita, and saw her some distance away, seated on a rock, smoking a cigarette. She inhaled with great deliberateness, each time holding the smoke carefully in her lungs for a moment before expelling it. She can't even smoke like other people, she thought. Then she saw that Grove had noticed her, too, and watched his expression cloud over with annoyance. "Come on!" he called. "The *fábrica,* before it gets dark."

He led them downward, along a narrow path between boulders and large ceiba trees with fat gray roots.

The *fábrica* was a vast wooden construction, built into the side hill on several levels, partly covered and partly roofless, a chaos of chutes and bins. In Indian file, with Grove leading, they picked their way among the mounds of coffee beans and got to a small office on the dim far side of the shed. A wizened, swarthy young man sat at a desk. "This is my foreman, Enrique Quiroga," said Grove, and they shook hands. Several workmen had taken up unmoving positions from which they could watch through the open door into the office. Grove seized one of several large sombreros that hung from a row of nails on the wall and threw it on his head at an angle. "I feel as though we were on our way to the captain's dinner," Day said to him.

"Not quite. Watch."

A few thin beams of late sunlight pierced the make-shift wall and slanted across the dark interior far above their heads. "Piranese," said Grove, walking ahead.

No one answered. "Come over here and look at this," he said.

Luchita was talking with the foreman. *"Hombre!"* she shouted.

In the corner, up and down, were dozens of webs, like hammocks carelessly slung between the two walls. An enormous black-and-yellow spider lay in each one.

"My God, their bodies are as big as plums!" cried Dr. Slade.

Crushing the crown of the sombrero in one hand, Grove made a long downward scooping gesture with it; the sticky membranes snapped. Then he held the hat up so they could see inside. Dr. Slade adjusted his glasses and stared.

"How many'd I get?"

"Seven or eight."

As Luchita came over to them, Grove bunched the crown together again. "Hold the shadow-maker a minute, will you?"

Dutifully she took it and carried it a few paces. One of the insects, climbing up to escape, touched her hand. She glanced down, screamed, and flung the hat away.

"Oh, I'll kill you, you lousy son of a bitch!" she cried, rushing at Grove to pound him with her fists.

"She hates them," he explained over her shoulder to Day, keeping her hands away from his face.

Behind the *fábrica* were several rows of thatched-roof huts where women chattered and children shrieked. They stood outside of one and looked in at the mud walls and dirt floor; an old woman lay on a pile of burlap sacks in one corner.

"Pretty primitive," said Dr. Slade. Day caught the inflection of criticism in his voice. Perhaps Grove noticed it also. "They're primitive people," he said. "Give them a bed and they put it out for the chickens to roost on. Give them money and they're drunk for two days."

"Still, they must have money sometimes," objected Dr. Slade.

"They don't see it from one year to the next. They get paid in scrip and buy their food at the company store on credit."

"I've read about the system," said Dr. Slade drily.

"They seem happy enough," Day began in an uncertain tone. She was ready to say anything which might forestall discussion of the subject: she knew Taylor.

At one side of the *fábrica*, under a large tree, there was a truck. "Enrique's giving us a lift back to the house," said Grove.

The bumpy trail led through scrub most of the way; it was almost dark when they arrived back at the house. Luchita had made a point of involving herself in a conversation with the foreman as soon as they had got into the truck. When it stopped she jumped down and disappeared.

The main courtyard of the monastery, terraced and open at one end, had not been changed. By daylight there was a view down through the cloistered garden and across the headlands to the curving river with its band of forest. In a corner on the highest terrace, glass walls had been built, and behind these they had dinner. The candles flickered in the breeze. Luchita was sleek and glowing in a close-fitting black gown. As she ate, she stared moodily out toward the invisible river, and when she spoke, her voice was sharp with emotion, alternately indignant and insolent.

"The poor child's still shaken," said Day to Grove. "Those spiders! Why did you do it?"

"Do what?" he cried disgustedly. "It's that very childishness she should be fighting against."

In principle Day agreed with him, but she raised her eyebrows to show disapproval. Looking at him, ruddy and beaming in the candlelight, she thought with faint repulsion: Men are all brutal with young girls. And even Taylor. He too had been sadistic to a small girl, but where had it been? And had he, really, or was it a false memory left over from her sickness?

All day long, here and there, at odd moments, something had been bothering her, and she had put off taking the time to see what it was. And now, as she suddenly came face to face with it, even as Luchita was refusing salad from the bowl the servant held in front of her, she knew in a flash that there was still an empty spot in the past.

She watched the man coming toward her with the salad bowl. Nothing of what was happening was understandable; it could as easily have been something completely different. Until she knew what had gone on before she could not fully accept what was going on now.

For one thing, it struck her as extremely strange that she should feel she knew Grove so well. His voice particularly—it was like a sound she had known all her life. There was something abnormal in the terrible familiarity she felt with its cadence and inflections. And then, What has he got against me? she wondered. Why is he practically vibrating with hostility? Several times during the day she had been nettled by his air of insolent triumph as he looked at her.

All at once she realized that Grove and Taylor were engaged in the argument she had been afraid they would have when they had stood among the workers' huts outside the *fábrica*.

"Yes, but what does the term 'human rights' mean? The American idea is based completely on the fact that Americans have always had more than their share." Grove fixed Dr. Slade with his forefinger. "Put them in the same position as the rest of the people in the world, and they'll understand soon enough that what they've had so far have been only privileges, not rights."

"But for your own protection, in a country like this," pursued Dr. Slade blandly, "it seems you'd do better to cut down the area of possible discontent, don't you think?"

Grove laughed. "Shall we go inside for coffee?" They rose from the table, leaving the candles to gutter in the rising breeze.

In the *sala* Grove stood facing Dr. Slade. "I know, I know," he said with impatience. "A liberal can't say no because he's got nothing to say yes to. But, Doctor, in political theory you keep up with research too."

Dr. Slade bridled. "I'm afraid I don't see the parallel."

They walked over and sat down by the coffee table. Luchita, seeing Grove come into the room, had stopped talking and had assumed a chastened attitude.

"Taylor! Listen to what Pepito said. Tell him, Luchita. It's marvelous!"

Luchita glanced apprehensively at Grove, who seemed amused by her sudden shyness.

"I don't know what's come over her. Ordinarily she doesn't mention the product of her childhood indiscretions," he said.

"Who's Pepito?" demanded Dr. Slade, still ruffled by what he considered Grove's unwarranted attack. But Luchita had risen silently, her face transformed by rage, and was already on her way out of the room. The sound of her heels tapping on the flagstones in the patio died away, and there was silence for an instant.

Finally Day said, "Well!" Grove went on to tell about Indian customs; there was no further reference to the angry exit. A half hour later he too got up, saying he had some work to do, and bade them good night.

They sat on in the *sala* for another few minutes, leafing through magazines in silence. Then, more with mutterings than with words, they agreed to get up and go to their room. Day took with her a copy of *Country Life* and one of *Réalités*. There was a barefoot Indian girl in their bedroom turning down the coverlets and laying out their bathrobes and slippers. She smiled at them and went out.

Dr. Slade stood by the window staring into the faintly lighted patio. Day had gone into the bathroom and was drawing water in the washbasin. He tried without success to remember the last occasion when he and Day had been together in bed. It was unimportant, and yet not knowing when or where it had been disturbed him.

At last she came into the room, radiant in a white peignoir. She walked over to him and put her arm through his. "Darling," he said, turning toward her to embrace her. The smell of her hair always reminded him of sunlight and wind. She did not raise her face to his.

He put his hand under her chin. "What's the matter?"

"Nothing very much," she said smiling; she pulled gently away from him and went to sit at the dressing table.

When he came out of the bathroom in his pajamas, she was sitting up with her sheet over her, looking at *Réalités*. She had tossed the copy of *Country Life* onto his bed. He lay down and stared for a minute at photographs of yew trees and English sitting rooms; then he turned off the lamp on his night table and let the magazine slide to the floor. A moment later Day clicked off her light; the room was in darkness. He heard her yawn faintly. After that there was silence, and then she spoke, tentatively: "Taylor."

"Yes," he murmured, forcing himself back into wakefulness. "What?"

"I wanted to ask you. Have you had any trouble trying to remember things? Since you were sick? Have you noticed anything?"

"A little." He was already wide-awake.

"I've got a big blank in my head. The whole trip is completely gone. It's awful."

"He mentioned the possibility of it. He said it would all come back."

"It's as though a whole section had been simply rubbed out."

"I know. I went through it yesterday," he said hesitantly. "This is one time when you've just got to be patient."

"You have no blank spots?" she insisted.

"I think they've all gone now." He fabricated a yawn; he hoped she would take the hint, and go to sleep. About his own situation he was not so happy as he had tried to appear. Very definitely there was a blind spot in his memory; he could recall nothing that had happened beyond the first two or three days on the ship out of San Francisco. But he had no intention of admitting it to Day; it would deprive her of the very support she most needed at the moment. Besides, he was convinced that between them they would be able to put together the jumbled pieces. Each day one or the other would supply more details, until the picture was complete for both of them.

He listened. She was still; he assumed she was asleep.

Words were deceptive, the very short ones most of all; she thought of the crucial importance of the two small words Taylor had just used: *he said*. He said the forgetfulness would quickly be dissipated. He said it was a result of something called Newbold's Disease. He said the best doctor in the capital had attended them. But would the faculty return intact? Taylor had never heard of Newbold's Disease. It was conceivable that a different doctor could have prescribed a treatment which would have obviated the aftereffects she was suffering. It was demoralizing to know that everything depended on the word of this particular young man. More than ever she distrusted him, and was annoyed only because she could find no more specific material to help her account for her feeling. It seemed to her that the mere fact of his having taken them in and having bothered to bring them all the way here to the ranch could be viewed in a suspicious light. There was a fundamental contradiction in his behavior: he had gone far out of his way to be hospitable and helpful, yet when she was with him she could not perceive even a glimmer of friendliness. He served his charm and courtesy mechanically; it was as if she and Taylor were paying guests and he a professional host. She was convinced that when he had left them an hour ago he had heaved a sigh of relief finally to be rid of them, free to get back to his own life. What his private world was like she could only surmise, but she was certain there was no corner in it for either her or Taylor; in that realm they counted as objects, not as people.

At some point in the night she had a dream. Or it was possible that she was partially awake, and was only remembering a dream? She was alone among the rocks on a dark coast beside the sea. The water surged upward and fell back languidly, and in the distance she heard surf breaking slowly on a sandy shore. It was comforting to be this close to the surface of the ocean and gaze at the intimate nocturnal details of its swelling and ebbing. And as she listened to the faraway breakers rolling up onto the beach, she became aware of another sound entwined with the intermittent crash of waves: a vast horizontal whisper across the bosom of the sea, carrying an ever-repeated phrase, regular as a lighthouse flashing: *Dawn will be breaking soon.* She listened a long time: again and again the scarcely audible words were whispered across the moving water. A great weight was being lifted slowly from her; little by little her happiness became more complete, and she awoke. Then she lay for a few minutes marveling at the dream, and once again fell asleep.

24

THE NEXT MORNING, some time after they had finished breakfast, Grove knocked on their door. Day, who had been sunbathing, pulled her bathrobe around her.

"I hate to invade your privacy like this," he said, striding into the patio where they sat. "Everything all right? Anything you need?" As they protested that all the details combined to make perfection, he settled back on a chaise longue and lit a cigarette. In a few minutes the purpose of his visit became clear: he had come to ask Dr. Slade to go with him to visit a nearby silver mine.

"A silver mine! Is that right?" said Dr. Slade with inflections of interest. "Why, I think I might enjoy it."

"Are you going *into* the mine?" Day inquired, looking intently at Grove.

He smiled. "It would be hard to see it from the outside."

"I hate places inside the earth!" she said with feeling, not removing her eyes from his.

"It's a common enough complaint," he told her, his smile even more bland. Suddenly she felt that he was encouraging her to make herself absurd beyond a point of dignified retreat, and so for a while she let the talk go on to other things. Then without warning she asked him, "Is this a modern mine?"

"It's safe, if that's what you mean. It's at least two centuries old. Very solid."

When Dr. Slade got up to leave and was about to follow Grove through the doorway, she said to him in a low voice, but loud enough so that he heard, "I wish you wouldn't go, Taylor."

He stopped and turned. "This is a fine time to tell me! I'll take it easy on the climbs and see you about twelve."

"Yes," she said tonelessly, waving her hand in his direction. He took it as a gesture of dismissal and went on.

When they were in the cloister of the main courtyard, Grove looked at him. "Day's full of anxieties, isn't she?"

"Not at all. She's unusually well balanced," said Dr. Slade. "Her nerves have been a little raw since she was sick, that's all."

Grove smiled tolerantly, shook his head. "Well, Doctor, she's *your* wife. You ought to know. On the other hand, that very intimacy you have might make it impossible for you to see what somebody else meeting her for the first time would see right off. You can't tell."

"I doubt that very much." Dr. Slade said with some force. Grove understood that he was not going to be receptive.

"Why should she be nervous?" he demanded. "She's completely recovered. You can see that."

Dr. Slade stopped walking. "But is she? She's got the same business I have." He tapped his forehead. "There are a whole lot of things she can't remember."

Grove snorted. "More likely it's imaginary. She knows she was out cold for a few days, so she feels the thread's been broken. I think you'll find she can remember, if you ask her the right questions."

158

They resumed walking, slowly. "I don't know," said Dr. Slade dubiously. "Certainly in my case it's real enough. There's a whole period that's just gone."

"Still missing!" Grove exclaimed.

Since he felt himself being encouraged to talk about it, during the drive he went into describing for Grove the extent of the lapse, using certain landmark dates and counting the days before and after them on his fingers. Between them they calculated that the lost time embraced a period of between thirteen and fifteen days.

"It's my main interest in life at the moment, getting back those days," said Dr. Slade, trying to smile. The hot wind cut violently across his face, making it hard to breathe.

"They'll come home, dragging their tails behind them." Grove was driving much too fast along the rough trail; he never moved his eyes from the track ahead.

Day, continuing her sunbath alone in the increasingly hot patio, went on striving to reconstruct key scenes whose details might call into being a fragment of the missing material. But it was like looking on the shore for yesterday's footprints. She held it against Taylor that he had gone out in spite of her having asked him not to: his absence left her alone with her preoccupation. She was certain that together they had a better chance of solving their difficulties than they ever could have separately.

When the maids came to make up the room she slipped on a shirt and some slacks, and wandered through the house to the front entrance. Outside in the road it seemed a little cooler. There were several dusty trails leading in various directions; the one she chose went along for a way beside the walls of the house and gardens. Soon it dipped and turned to the left. In spite of the heat she continued slowly, scuffing the dust with her sandals as she went along. Then she turned and went back toward the ranch more quickly than she had come. Once in the courtyard, she heard voices coming from the *sala*, and looked in.

"You should have seen it," Taylor told her. "There were brooks of cyanide everywhere."

She laughed shortly and took the cocktail Grove was holding out to her. "That's what I need, some good cyanide."

The dining room was a small museum of pre-Columbian art; its walls were peppered with niches that held masks and sculptures. Grove had wanted to eat here, insisting that it was too hot to be outside. There was a discussion then with Luchita, who protested that the air conditioning made it too cold to be in the dining room. As they sat down to lunch she brought it up again.

"And besides that, you give us vichyssoise with ice in it," she complained.

"Ah, the old teahead freeze. It's hot in here." Grove looked to Day for support.

"It feels just right to me," she said lightly, at the same time twining her legs together, for it seemed uncomfortably chilly.

"Delightful," said Dr. Slade.

"You've got a jacket on," Day told him, and stopped. "What god is that?" she inquired presently, pointing to the huge stone figure that towered at the far end of the room.

Grove glanced at the statue with respect. "That's Xiuloc, god of the life force. They called him the Father of Boils. He weighs fourteen tons."

"I'd have thought a good deal more," said Dr. Slade morosely; he considered it an absurdity to surround a dining table with grimacing faces and snarling muzzles.

"That's the point," Grove told him. "The stone is porous. They broke their boils on it and the stone sucked out the pus."

"Oh," said Day, looking down at her vichyssoise.

"God of the life force," repeated Dr. Slade, as if considering the idea.

"How'd you ever corral all these things?" she asked Grove.

"Everything was dug up on our own land somewhere. The government got the big ones. But there's one mammoth in the studio you've got to see."

"You won't sleep for two weeks if you look at that. I'm telling you the truth," Luchita warned her, speaking with great seriousness.

"I can't wait," she said to Grove. "What is it?"

"Just a divinity. But it's got snakes and spiders in it, and that bothers her."

What am I doing here? she asked herself. It was absurd to be sitting in this glacial room with these two disconnected young people; to prolong the visit would be senseless. She suspected that it was going to be hard to spur Taylor to action. Perhaps a scene would not be necessary, but she was prepared to produce one if he demurred. At least there was satisfaction in knowing that she was no longer of two minds about it.

Immediately after lunch, while Luchita and Dr. Slade were having coffee in the cloister, Grove took her into the room where the big statue was. The light behind it came down from windows high above; she had a strong impression that the object was alive and conscious. A gigantic piece of stone, waiting. Whether it was decorated with snakes and spiders, or hearts and skulls, was beside the point. It was the stone itself that was alive.

161

From somewhere above their heads came the desperate buzzing of a solitary fly as it banged against a pane of glass. The air in the room was hot and still. The longer they sat without speaking, the more importance the statue would assume.

"I think Luchita and I see it the same way," she finally said. "These Indian things down here give me the shudders."

"Don't you think it's a beauty?" Grove demanded.

"It's magnificent. But I wouldn't want to live anywhere near it. I don't even like to touch these things." Her tone had become one of apology; then it resumed its natural sound. "I think these were pretty terrible civilizations, don't you?"

"Terrible compared to what? Sit down here on the couch where you can look up at it. It has a sense of balance all its own."

She laughed and obligingly seated herself. "It's much worse from here, of course. But you said, Compared to what? Well, to our own Christian civilization, for instance."

Abruptly he sat down beside her. "The one thing Christianity has given the world is a lesson in empathy. Jesus's words are a manual on the technique of putting yourself in the other's place."

"Is that what they are?" If he was hoping to make her angry, she would disappoint him.

"Your husband worries too much about you," he went on, as though continuing the conversation.

"Worries about me?" she exclaimed, astonished.

"I suppose he's concerned about your aftereffects, your hangover of amnesia."

"That's ridiculous," she said, annoyed to hear that they had discussed her. "It's not permanent, is it?"

"No, no." He said only that, and then there was the sound of the fly's agonized attempt to escape. They sat there.

Finally he spoke. "You have to work at it, you know. For instance, when we were out on the terrace, up in the capital, you spoke about coming out of the customhouse at Puerto Farol, and from the way you described it, it seemed like a very sharp and detailed memory."

"Yes," she said uncertainly. The picture as she saw it now was not sharp and detailed at all; it was like remembering a photograph she had once looked at rather than an experience she had lived through.

"You know the part I mean." His voice had overtones of impatience. "When the side of the building and the signboard seemed to buckle as you were falling, and the water in the harbor was flowing like a river? And the uprooted palm trees lying along the waterfront?"

She shut her eyes for a few seconds. When she opened them again her heart was beating violently. Without saying anything she shook her head slowly back and forth.

"Anyway," he went on, "it's not what you saw or thought you saw at that moment, but the fact that those clear memories came right in the middle of your blocked-out period."

She was silent for a moment. Her heart still pounding, she got up quietly and said, "Couldn't we go back?" Without looking again at the statue, she walked toward the door leading out to the cloister.

In the *sala* there was no sign of Luchita or Dr. Slade, and the coffee tray had been cleared away. "Taylor must have gone for his siesta," she said. "I'm going in too, if you don't mind."

"It's hot today," he told her. "The end of the dry season it gets like this."

Taylor had told her about the end of the dry season in that part of the world, how all of nature seemed to be straining to pull a little moisture out of the sky, until one could feel the tension in everything, and the scorpions came out and the lightning flashed more each night, and human nerves grew taut. As she lay back on her pillow, with Taylor snoring gently on the other bed, she tried to find the reason why it had been such an unpleasant experience to have Grove remind her of the arrival in Puerto Farol. It had been like hearing her own dream being told by someone who could tell it far better than she ever could. A few days ago the mention of it on the terrace in the city had been bad, but today's reminder had been infinitely worse, because his unexpected inclusion of the forgotten details of the water in the harbor pouring out to sea and the broken palm trees had given her a terrifying sensation of being dependent upon him, as if she would remember whatever he chose to have her remember. This was manifestly nonsense. She determined not to speak of it to Taylor, who already was treating her with a little of the condescension one shows to invalids.

She listened: the dry wind bore the sound of singing insects as it blew through the patio, and the long, hard leaves of the pandanus bumped one against the next. It would have made her happy to lean across the space between the two beds and take Taylor by the arm. When he was awake she would say, I want to go tomorrow morning.

She sat up. There was no question of relaxing enough to be able to doze off, and if she could not sleep she did not want to be lying there. A walk, even in the burning mid-afternoon sun, would be preferable. She could try a different road—one that might take her to a vantage point where she could see the entire ranch from above.

A few minutes later she stepped out into the wind. There was not a person in sight on any of the roads. The monastery was prolonged by walls for a great distance at each end; she turned to the right and followed the wall. Soon she came to an open door. She peered through and saw some avocado trees. There was a primitive hut back in the deep shade. Turkeys pecked at the dust. One of the maids came out of the hut, caught sight of her, and waved.

She walked on. In the air was the simple odor of the dusty plains, tinged occasionally with a whiff of plant life from the jungle below. The road led upward, over the crest of a small hill. On each side was a living fence of high cactus, and each plant was entirely wrapped in a thick coating of spiderwebs that quivered in the wind. The dust in the road was thick and satiny; no tracks were visible on its recently deposited surface. And in the maze of webs there was nothing but an occasional dry twig or scrap of insect. Yet she repeatedly found herself staring carefully into the tattered gossamer world, as if somewhere inside might be lurking something which would translate itself into the answer to an as yet unformulated question.

The bare hillside had a few rocks and prickly shrubs scattered over it. There was nothing to look at. But the mere act of walking made it easier to accept the fact that she was only waiting for Taylor to finish his nap.

Up here the whole landscape looked scraggy and desolate; its leafless trees and slag-colored expanses made her want to shut her eyes. Whichever way she looked, it was the same: gray and burned out—a landscape imitating death. But when she got to the crest of the hill she found that on the other side it overlooked a bend in the river valley. The tufted tops of the big trees lay steeply below, and in the middle distance she could see stretches of the river as it wandered through the jungle, back and forth across the valley. From where she stood there was no sign of human presence—only the wasteland around her, the valley below, and beyond that more wasteland, rising on and on, to shadows of high mountains on the farthest horizon. After she had stood a while she went back, feeling frustrated.

In the bedroom he was still asleep. She continued into the bathroom and, leaving the door partly open, took a noisy shower. When she came out, he was stirring.

"You're so lucky to be able to sleep that way. Do you want me to ring for tea?"

"I suppose. I've been sweating. It's hot in here."

Ten minutes later, while he was eating an éclair, she began. "You know what I'd like?" she said. "I'd like to pack my things tonight and leave tomorrow morning."

He stared at her. "That seems like rather short notice, doesn't it? They'll think something's wrong."

It annoyed her to hear him include Luchita along with Grove, as if she carried some weight in his household. "Plenty's wrong, and it's all with him. I could fly out of my skin."

"Day, you can't just walk out on people. How do you know what they've got planned for us?"

"Planned!" she cried piteously.

"We can't do it. We've got to give them a little notice."

"I really hate it here," she said in a small, pathetic voice. "I'd like to be in a hotel."

"I got to know him a little this morning," Dr. Slade

said meditatively. "You can't help liking the boy. He's had a pretty tough time."

She was contemptuous. "Oh, stop it! He was brought up in the lap of luxury."

"What's that got to do with it? There are other things besides comfort and financial security."

"You'd never guess it."

He shrugged. "You want to be harsh on him, that's all." Then he turned and saw the anxiety in her face. "Why don't we compromise and tell them at dinner we've got to leave day after tomorrow?"

"But definitely? No matter what?"

"Well, of course definitely."

She was silent a moment. "That makes another forty or more hours to get through. God!"

"I wish you'd just relax," he told her.

By dinnertime it had cooled off enough so that they were able to eat in the courtyard under the stars. About halfway through the meal Dr. Slade cleared his throat, and she knew he was going to begin. "Grove, Day and I have been talking it over, and we feel we've got to be getting on." There was a long period of protestation and mutual flattery; she was aware of what Taylor was going through, and she felt sorry for him.

Luchita, looking very pale and sophisticated, had finished her steak and lighted one of her aromatic cigarettes. Her humor was better tonight; from time to time she looked derisively at Grove as he attempted to persuade Dr. Slade to put off his departure. What a rude little bitch she is, Day thought. She might as well have been saying aloud, This isn't what he tells *me*.

It was understood that Grove would drive them to the station at San Felipe and put them on the train for the capital. As they went across the cloister into the *sala,* Grove added, "Luchita's going up anyway on Friday."

Quick as a lizard Luchita turned in the doorway. "Oh, I am?" she cried hoarsely. "You think I am? On the train?"

Day sat down in the place indicated for her, while Grove piled cushions behind her back. She watched the girl closely. Grove turned to her and said in an offhand manner, "Luchita, do you remember a restaurant near the Place de l'Alma called A la Grenouille de Cantal?" Looking earnestly at her, he waited for the reply. And Day was first astonished and then incensed, with the result that she felt impelled to side with the girl. It was a shamefully unequal struggle; Luchita wilted, melted, as if an invisible blow had been struck her. After a moment she said in an almost inaudible voice, "Yes, Vero."

A little while later, when she had the opportunity, Day said in an aside to Grove, "You seem to have *all* the answers."

"Not all," he said, looking carefully at her.

She had hoped to keep the hard edge of her voice covered, but she knew it had cut through; his look at her had been swift and keen. And his astuteness in discerning the hostility she had meant to keep hidden surprised her; it ran counter to certain key prejudices she had regarding him.

When they got to the bedroom and the door was shut behind them, Day stood motionless. "You see what I mean about him?" she demanded.

"He and the girl were on the outs, that's all."

It seemed useless to discuss it. From her bed, propped up against the pillows, she watched Dr. Slade as he shuffled about the room in his bathrobe. Soon he got into the other bed, took off his wristwatch, and reached out to lay it on the night table.

"Has it ever occurred to you," she said, looking at him steadily, "to ask yourself *why* he brought us here?"

He looked incredulous. "*Why?* My God, girl, he's just being hospitable! How can you ask *why?*"

"I can ask anything," she said.

25

IT WAS TWENTY-FIVE minutes past eight. From her bed Day heard the rustling of small birds in the patio's shrubs. Because the air was so still she could hear even the distant sounds from the kitchen: a pail being set down, the chatter of women, a door slamming. Taylor lay on his side, asleep. Tomorrow at this time I'll be on the train, she thought, wondering how she would get through the enormous day of waiting that lay ahead of her.

In the dim bathroom as she washed, she was telling herself that each hour equaled about four per cent of the time left, which meant that every fifteen minutes one per cent would tick by. At first her reckoning made the time seem finite and bearable, but after several carefully spaced glances at her watch, she understood that fifteen minutes was a long period of time.

During the course of the morning she gave several small things to the chambermaid to wash out for her, explaining that she must have them all back by evening.

Between bouts of packing she sunbathed in the patio with Taylor. Just before they went in to lunch, the girl brought all the clothing back, washed, dried and ironed. "Of course. Everything dries in two minutes in this climate," said Taylor.

At one o'clock they assembled in the *sala* for cocktails. Now there was no sign of friction between Grove and Luchita. "One last round before we go into that icebox," Grove advised, pouring out the drinks for everyone but Luchita, who was still sipping her first.

"Wise girl," commented Dr. Slade. "You don't ever drink much, do you?"

"It makes me feel sick," she told him.

Sitting at the table directly across from Luchita, Day had the opportunity of examining her at close range. What she saw struck her as extraordinarily unpleasant: for the first time in her life she felt she was looking at a zombie. The girl's eyes were almost closed, and a gigantic, meaningless smile lay over her face. When she was spoken to, she appeared to have difficulty finding her voice in order to reply. At least, thought Day, this beatific state augured a quiet meal.

"Well, so this is our last lunch together," said Dr. Slade, spooning up his gazpacho. "It's been so pleasant I hate to get out of the rut. This is certainly one part of the trip I'll never forget."

Day tittered and turned red. Dr. Slade did not seem to have heard. Luchita stared at her, suddenly wide-eyed; then she put her head back and looked down from her own remote heights upon the antics of the alcohol drinker.

"You've missed a great chance, you know, Day." Grove pointed a cigarette at her. "I'd have taken you into San Felipe. A local fiesta."

Day had brought her cocktail in with her; now she sipped it. "Don't tell me," she pleaded. "I don't want to know what I'm missing."

While the others talked, she was busy calculating that already about twenty-two per cent of her time had gone past.

"How about it, Day? You put off your trip and take in the fiesta?"

"You're not serious?"

"Yes."

"Of course we're not going to put off anything. We're leaving tomorrow morning." She laughed in order to seem less ungracious and looked toward Taylor, fearful that he might yet allow the departure to be placed in question. She would not have been astonished at that moment if Grove had spoken out suddenly, declaring that it would be impossible for them to leave. Then she understood that the danger was past and that he would say no more about it.

As they got up from the table, Dr. Slade put his hand on Grove's arm. "Now if you'll forgive me this once, I'll cut the coffee and make straight for my bed."

"Yes," Day said. "I'm sleepy too."

Trying to keep out of the stinging sunlight, they walked slowly along the cloister toward their room. Grove called after them, "Tea in your room at five?"

"Lovely!" said Day. Then she muttered, "Breakfast and tea are the best meals in *this* house. I thought the lunch would never end."

"He makes his drinks too damned strong," Dr. Slade declared.

The curtains were drawn against the glare of the patio. "Will it bother you if I go on packing?" she asked him. He was wrapping his beach bathrobe around him. "Go

171

right ahead," he said. Then, "Whew!" he exclaimed fervently as he fell onto the bed.

For a while she moved aimlessly around the darkened room, carrying objects from one place to another. Finally it became clear to her that everything was packed except the things that had to be left out until the last moment. Common sense told her to stay in the room, where there was no risk of running into Grove and having to engage in conversation with him, but the prospect of lying quietly in the gloom for two or three hours was more than she could face. She was too nervous to read. There was nothing to do but go outside.

It was unlikely that Grove would be wandering around the servants' garden at this hour. There was always life in the neighborhood of the kitchen, and it was soothing to watch people in the act of performing simple tasks. She went out through the big door and followed the road that went along beside the wall. When she came to the garden door, she pushed it open and stepped inside.

At once she had the impression that the place was deserted. The turkeys were there, furrowing the dust with their stiff tailfeathers, and somewhere behind one of the huts farther back in the shade a dog yapped; but she did not hear a human sound.

Leading back to the kitchen door was a long pergola with a trelliswork top where flowering vines drooped. She walked along slowly, marveling at the silence of the afternoon. As she came out into sunlight, she saw on a flagstone at her feet the remains of a small bonfire. Several sheets of typewritten paper had been partially burned; the black-edged, irregular yellow scraps lay beside her foot. She craned her neck a bit and, with her head on one side, looked at what was written there. The word "scaffolding" caught her eye. Then she straightened and walked on to the kitchen door.

There was no sound inside but the steady cheerful dripping of a tap into a sink full of water. The room was very bright; there were glass bricks in the ceiling. She walked in front of the enormous fireplace. It was, of course, the hour of the siesta, when everyone managed to crawl away and lose consciousness for an hour or two, but she would expect to find at least one maid somewhere about. As she continued into the pantry, her movements became stealthy; she felt she had had no right to go through the kitchen. Surely Grove would consider it a kind of trespassing. In the dining room's cold vault the silence was at its most strident. She went quickly through without glancing at the grinning faces. There was no one in the courtyard. A hammock had been slung across between two pillars, and a book lay open in it, face down. The wind hissed among the thousands of twigs in the lemon tree and pushed the tendrils of overhanging vines out to touch her.

When she came to the turning that led to their room, she hesitated an instant, and then continued straight ahead to the front door. This time she took the road that led downward toward the river. On the promontory that was visible from where they had sat at lunch there were a few low shaggy trees where buzzards perched, and a small partially ruined chapel. This was where the workmen were installing the swimming pool; half of it would be shaded by the apse and the rest would be in the sunlight. She could see the mounds of earth and the wheelbarrows in front of the baroque façade, but no workmen.

It gave her pleasure to scuff her feet through the thick dust, raising a long cloud that moved off behind her across the empty land. The dust was everywhere on her;

she thought voluptuously of the shower she would take on returning. It would be more fun to have something visible to wash off.

When the road began to descend too steeply she climbed up over the rocks at the side to get a view across the highest branches of the trees that loomed ahead, and if possible to get a glimpse of the river. Then she stood there staring out at the savage landscape. Directly below her, half covered by trees, was the red roof of the coffee *fábrica*. The ribbon of jungle wound deliberately through the barren country, covering great distances back and forth across the valley; of the river itself there was no sign. Only one more meal to sit through, she reflected with satisfaction.

It was not quite ten to five when she got back to the room, but Taylor had already drunk his tea and gone back to sleep. The tray was there, the teapot empty. He would always drink it while it was hot, without waiting for her, no matter when they brought it. But she was annoyed with Grove. He had said five; here she was, just in time, and there was no tea for her.

Taylor was asleep on his back. It looked like an uncomfortable position, but there was no question of waking him to make him change it. After she had taken her shower she lay out flat on her bed, hoping to relax for a few minutes. Occasionally she rose and walked slowly around the room. When it was twilight she went through the curtained door and into the rosy gray light of the patio. She stood, feeling the slight wind go past.

When the stars are really out I'll wake him up, she thought. With the trip in view it was good that he was sleeping so long. If she changed for dinner now, he could have the bathroom to himself when he got up.

A half hour later, when she was dressed to go in for cocktails, she wandered once more out into the patio and stared up at the sky. The wind had dropped; there were a few stars, but most of them were hidden by great masses of distant cumulus, still white with daylight from behind the horizon. As she watched, tongues of lightning moved between the clouds, and they glowed and flickered with yellow light from deep inside.

She went back in and, opening one of Taylor's valises, took out a pack of playing cards. She sat sideways on her bed and unthinkingly began to play a kind of solitaire she had not thought of since her childhood. Suddenly she made her decision. "Taylor!" she said. She looked over at him and thought she saw him breathe more deeply. "Come on. It's seven-thirty."

His eyes were still shut, and his hands were folded comfortably on his chest.

"Taylor!" she cried. She leaned across and seized his arm, shook it roughly. Already she was certain that nothing was going to rouse him. She jumped up. Standing directly over him, looking down upon his head, feeling his forehead, she thought: He's going to die. This time he's going to die.

It was not much later when she pushed the wall button to call the maid. Then she felt his pulse, and sat intent on the insistent throbs beneath the ball of her finger. There was no knock at the door; she rang again. In the bathroom she dampened a towel and brought it to put around his head. As she pushed the folds of wet linen against his hair she saw that she should have wrung out the towel much more firmly. The water trickled onto the pillow. If by now no one had come in answer to her call, no one was going to come, because the house was empty.

175

She went in the direction of the corridor. The lights were burning there. When she got to the far side of the courtyard she saw Grove standing inside the doorway of the *sala*.

26

TOGETHER THEY STOOD in the room looking at Taylor, Grove nodding his head slowly as he studied the inert form that lay there.

"Can't we call a doctor?" she said finally.

"I'm afraid he wouldn't thank us for calling in Dr. Solera." He smiled wryly at her. "It's nothing, nothing," he added almost impatiently. "If he doesn't come around by midnight I'll give him a shot."

He led her into the *sala*, where he handed her a double vodka martini.

"I'm really master of the house tonight," he said with relish. "I let the whole staff go to the fiesta. Everybody."

"I noticed the quiet. You mean there are really just the four of us in the house tonight?"

"Three," he said, rising to take his cigarette case from the mantel. "Luchita went up this afternoon." He smiled ingenuously. "You were wrong. You see what happened. She took the station wagon."

She felt her eyes growing wide with dismay. To offset the impression that might make, she slowly let her face expand into a delighted grin.

"No trains for Luchita!" she said, trying to laugh, shaking her head. Suddenly she knew he was at her again, studying each muscle of her face as it moved from one expression to another. I can't let him see I'm afraid, she kept thinking. It was as though he were waiting for her to betray herself.

"Who's getting dinner?" she said.

"I am. We are. If you don't mind helping me."

"No," she said, trying to sound pleasant.

"I'll show you the kitchen."

In her mind's eye she saw the whitewashed walls, the black beams overhead, and the huge fireplace. "Have you installed gadgets?" she asked him. "Or do you use the old kitchen, the way it was?"

"It's not old. It's just smoky." He was eying her in a curious manner, perhaps a little in the way a painter would look at a model he was about to begin sketching. "It looks old, I admit. It's an addition from the turn of the century."

Feeling the wind sweep all at once into the room and inundate her with its sweet forest smell, she looked around toward the door. "What's happening out there?"

"It's capricious this time of year," he said. "Off and on, up and down."

The wind had brought the wilderness into the room; her ear now focused on the sounds it was making in the vegetation outside.

"You never talk about yourself," she told him, as he handed her a second double martini.

"I'm always talking about myself."

"I mean your life. When you were a boy, for instance."

He laughed scornfully, but although she waited, he still said nothing.

She rose. "I've got to get something to put around my shoulders. The wind's blowing right on me."

He did not offer to go with her. As she hurried along toward the bedroom, she found herself marveling that she should be able to go on talking while Taylor lay unconscious. It seemed to help prove the truth of a suspicion she had long entertained: people could not really get very close to one another; they merely imagined they were close. (It was not a relapse, merely a part of the tapering off, Grove had said. There was no danger.)

She hunted out the stole she wanted and put it around her shoulders. "Don't disturb him. The thing is to leave him alone." She went over to Taylor's bed and took away the wet towel from around his head. With a fresh towel she dried the strands of damp hair as well as she could. His breathing was regular, slow and profound, and his face looked neither flushed nor pale. It seemed cruel to leave him alone in order to go and sit in the *sala* making meaningless conversation.

As she turned the corner of the cloister, she glanced down the long corridor that lost itself in a dim confusion of plants and furniture. A man in a white shirt had stood for a second at the far end before stepping ahead into the darkness of the courtyard; he did not reappear.

Grove had turned on some jazz and was stretched out full-length on the floor. She went in, and since he did not get up, she stood a moment and then sat down in a chair by the door, where the sound of the music was not so deafening. When the final cymbal crash had announced the end of the piece, he rose and turned off the machine.

"Sometimes I like it so loud it hurts," he told her.

"You said there was no one in the house," she began. "But there's somebody out there. I just saw him."

"Where?" he demanded, staring at her. The idea hovered in her mind that he might be afraid.

178

"Way down at the end of the colonnade. He went out into the bushes."

"There's a night guard on, down at the generator. He must have come up for something."

"I was surprised," she said, laying her hand over her heart. "I'm on edge, naturally."

"Yes." It was clear that he was thinking about something different. "Of course." Then he turned to her abruptly. "If you're worrying about the doctor, don't."

She looked at him almost tearfully for an instant. "Of course I'm worried!" she cried.

"But you're a fool—" he raised his hand—"if you let him take that trip tomorrow, no matter how he feels."

"I'm for calling your doctor right now." She felt certain of being able to manage the doctor; he would give his permission, and Taylor could go. "Is he so bad?"

"He's not so good; I can tell you that."

"At least he's a doctor," she said reproachfully.

"You don't want another drink, do you? Let's go out and get dinner. We can talk while we work."

As he piloted her through the dim dining room she was telling herself that from the instant they went through the doorway into the pantry she must behave as though she were seeing everything for the first time. Halfway through the pantry she said, "This is an older wing, isn't it?"

He was not listening. "There are some mangoes and papayas in the icebox that have got to be cut up." They were in the kitchen; she looked up at the vaulted beams.

Grove filled a large pot, and another small one, with water, set them on the stove, and lighted the gas burners. "Now we've got direct contact," he said under his breath. While the water heated, she helped him cut up the fruit

179

on the big center table. Then she stood back against the sink and watched while he opened tins and packets and began silently to stir up a sauce over the flame.

"Do you think Luchita's gone for good?" she asked him.

He looked up in surprise. "Why would I think that? She didn't run away."

"Why don't you marry her, Grove?" she said softly.

"You're serious?" He stopped stirring for an instant and saw that she was. "You've seen her," he said, emptying a box of spaghetti into the cauldron of boiling water.

"Oh, marry her, for God's sake! What's the matter with you?"

Turning to the smaller vessel he held up his arm and let some of the sauce drip from the spoon back into the pot, watching it carefully as it fell. "In this country," he told her, speaking slowly, "they say you might as well make a political speech as give unwanted advice. Nobody's going to listen in either case."

She dropped her cigarette into the sink behind her. "Well, I can tell you, you'll never be happy until you do what you know's the right thing. That's what life's about, after all."

"What life's about!" he cried incredulously. "What *is* life about? Yes. What's the subject matter?" He stirred the sauce. "It's about who's going to clean up the shit."

"I don't know what you mean," she said, her voice hostile.

"The work's got to be done. If *you* don't want to do it, you've got to be able to make somebody else do it. That's what life's about. Or isn't that the way you like to hear it?"

She hesitated. "I don't understand. You seem like a ma-

ture man. Why you haven't outgrown all this, I mean. If
you were ten years younger it wouldn't be so surprising."
She would have enjoyed being able to say "so repulsive,"
because that was the way she felt, but to risk a break
would be a kind of abdication; she must stay with him
and prove, at least to herself, that she was not afraid of
him. Turning her head so he would not see the expression of distaste she knew was on her face, she finally said,
"But, isn't it boring eventually? All this animosity, year
after year, hating, hating? How do you keep up interest?"

"Life makes it easy. You don't have to worry about
that."

She shrugged. "It's not my problem."

"Only a drooling idiot would tell his troubles to a
woman," he said suddenly, with some bitterness.

"Troubles?" She eyed him as she lighted another cigarette. "You have troubles?"

His face darkened; he studied the sauce more closely.
"Yes. I have troubles." He had said the word without
choosing it, but now he seemed to be considering its
meaning.

She looked at him and believed him. "I'm sorry," she
said. "But whatever they are, I have a feeling you'll get
them behind you. It's a question of making up your
mind."

He seemed to stiffen. "In what way?"

"I mean setting your mind to putting them behind
you."

He wheeled to face her, and she saw with a cold dread
that he had had his eyes shut for the past few seconds;
they were still shut as he turned. When he opened them,
he opened his mouth as well, and laughed once. It
sounded like a young dog trying to bark.

"*Abajo* San Felipe!" he cried. "I'm no cook." She had the impression now that he had clambered back inside himself and shut the door.

"I didn't have to let them all go," he went on. "It seemed like a cheap way of reinforcing goodwill between master and servant. You have to keep shoring it up, you know. It wears away like a sea wall. Why don't we sit down right here? Or would you rather put everything on trays and take it into the dining room?"

She went on looking at him, aware suddenly that there was a shadowy bond between them. It was at that instant she first felt the cold impact of physical fear. And for some hidden reason she hoped never to discover, he was afraid of her.

They sat down at a long marble-topped table near the fireplace. The smell of garlic and spices was in the steam that rose from the sauce, but she had no appetite for it when he passed it to her. It had been a fraction of a second that she had looked into his eyes as they opened after having been focused on an inner world of torment, but she had been caught up and drawn into orbit along with him. By the time she had thought: I am I, it was finished, yet for that flash the difference between them had been next to nothing. It was a fact as much as the water dripping from the tap (now into a shallow dish) or the electric clock whirring on top of the refrigerator, or the smoky façade of the chimney above the fireplace.

After the first few mouthfuls she found it easier to eat. He told her several unlikely stories about the abbot of the monastery; she listened and watched him, remembering that at least time was going past. The trouble with Grove was, she thought, trying to be objective about him for a minute, that it was impossible to be relaxed in his presence: he was too desperate and final in his manner.

"There's always a pan of ice cream in the fridge for me," he said when they had finished. "I hope to hell it's there tonight. They get excited by fiestas. Anything can happen."

He got up and peered into the freezing compartment. "It's here," he announced. "Would you like some?"

She let him heap it into a bowl for her. "We'll eat it by the fire," he told her.

Reclining on piles of cushions in the familiar *sala*, she felt a little better, although she longed to get to her own room. He turned on the tape recorder; this time the jazz was a scarcely audible background.

They talked sporadically. Betweentimes the music went on playing. Finally the soft curtain of jazz had become empty silence; the machine continued to run. She could hear the long trills of the night insects in the higher branches of the lemon tree outside. Now and then a languorous stirring of the wind reached her where she sat.

Grove was up, had stopped the tape recorder, was spinning the tape ahead. "I have a wonderful jungle sequence somewhere on here. Just sounds at night." He started the tape, turned up the volume, and the dry, metallic song of the forest night filled the room.

"Beautiful," she said. After a suitable period of listening, she stood up.

"He's all right. Believe me," he told her, rising. "The thing is to let him wake up by himself. If he's hungry, or you want anything, my room's the last one on the right going down, at the end."

"Thank you." She was too tired to think of anything else to say.

27

EVERYTHING WAS THE SAME in the room: the lighted floor lamp, the curtains across the doorway into the little garden, the nightgown draped over the cowhide back of the chair. Dr. Slade, however, was not in the bed. She saw the depression in the mattress, and the flattened part of the pillow where his head had been lying. It was too much what she had hoped for; it could not be true. "Taylor," she called softly, standing beside the bathroom door.

No sound. She opened the door a crack; it was dark inside. She pushed open the door and stared into the empty bathroom. She pulled aside the curtains and went out into the patio. It was fairly dark out there, but she could see the whitewashed walls all around, and the sharp black forms of the plants against them. There was no one there.

Back in the room standing near the foot of her bed, she turned slowly, looking at each wall in succession. There was no point in going to the door and shouting his name up and down the cloister; nevertheless she stepped outside for an instant and cried "Taylor!" once, into the darkened courtyard. A moment later she began to walk swiftly along under the arches toward the far open end of the cloister. The last door had a sliver of light under it. She knocked four times, quickly.

It seemed a long time before Grove, wearing a white bathrobe, stepped outside and shut the door behind him.

They stood in the dark. He waited, and so she spoke.

"He's gotten up and gone out of the room. I don't know where to look for him."

He knotted the belt of the bathrobe tighter about his waist. "He's somewhere around. He won't have gone far."

"Somewhere around," she repeated without conviction. "In the dark?" She gestured with an arm, indicating the vast unlighted expanse of the courtyard. "He shouldn't be wandering around. Suppose he's delirious or walking in his sleep?"

He patted her on the shoulder. "Why don't you just go to bed? He'll be back. He probably wanted a little air."

This was more than she could take. "Are you out of your mind?" she cried. "I've got to find him."

"Feel free to go anywhere. There's generally a light switch on the right inside each door. I don't think you'll find him. As you say, he's not likely to be standing around in a dark house." He stepped toward the doorway.

There was a long silence. "I see," she said. "I thought you might be willing to help."

He did not reply, merely stood there with his hand on the doorknob.

At last he's showing his true colors, she thought. She listened to the wind in the vines. A rooster crowed nearby.

"If he's not in the house, he's gone out," he said. "If he's gone out he'll be back. He's not a child."

"The fact that he's been sick, the fact that only an hour ago he was still unconscious, none of that means anything to you?"

He opened his door a crack and started in. "It doesn't because it's irrelevant. I'd advise you to go back and get into bed."

"You're incredible!" she told him, but her voice was so tight with rage that she doubted he heard her. In her anger she spun around and began to walk very fast. The sound of her heeltaps on the stones struck her as ridiculous even as she heard his door shut. Her fancy was beset with images of pummeling him, clawing his face, kicking him; the black hatred he had aroused spread to the house itself and the countryside around it, and she found herself at the main entrance door, which she opened. She stood there, looking out at the road and the trees swimming in the moonlight. Suddenly she felt certain that Taylor was out here—not in the house.

First she went to the gate that led into the garden. It was unlocked. Inside, the huts were all dark, and the thatch of their roofs was mottled with tiny patches of moonlight that sifted down through the high trees. She stepped uncertainly ahead into the gloom, and then she stopped moving and listened. What she heard in the distance sounded like a drum beating a fast, irregular rhythm. The generator, she thought, and there was a man on duty there. She walked on into the tunnel of shadow. When the avenue of trees and huts had finished, she came out into an open space, and there was a flight of steps leading down. The sound was very loud here; she could see a little building in the bushes below, but no light. The moonlight was bright on the steps. Until she got around to the other side of the cabin and walked under the banana plants that grew in front of it she did not hear the radio. Then she saw a man squatting just outside the open door, his transistor on the ground in front of him. He grunted, jumped up and snapped on a light in the doorway; a tawny Indian youth in a visored cap stared at her with suspicion. She smiled, but could think of no explanation to give for her sudden intrusion.

The boy did not return the smile. Instead, he called out, "Señor Torny!"

There was the sound of heavy boots coming nearer on the other side of the plants. A tall young man in cowboy uniform moved into view, and remained looking impassively in her direction for what seemed a long time. Like the nasty one in a Western, she thought. The Indian boy did not move again. Suddenly the cowboy spoke in a low thin voice, and she jerked her head up in surprise. His English was perfect.

"Looking for something in particular or just taking a walk?"

"Oh, I heard the sound and I came down," she said, knowing that what she was saying was absurd, unconvincing. He still waited, and an idea came to her. "I think you were right in the beginning. I did want something."

She waited again. "Yes," he finally said.

"What I really needed but didn't dare hope for was a ride into San Felipe."

"You mean tonight, now?"

"That's what I meant."

He stepped toward her. "I'd do it, baby, but the truck isn't mine."

She hesitated. "I just wanted to get to a doctor."

Again he merely looked at her.

She was not certain how he was going to react, but she went ahead anyway. "It would be worth a hundred dollars to me to get there."

"I see." Now he stared at the ground.

Eventually he looked up at her. "The problem's still the same, but I'll risk it. When do you want to go?"

"Right now."

"I'll have to get the keys. Wait there." He turned away.

187

The sound of his boots on the gravel became fainter. She moved aimlessly around in the open space in front of the banana plants while the Indian boy stared at her. Now and then she felt a compulsion to go back to the bedroom: Taylor could be there waiting. But she did not believe it, and she would not go into the house again until she had Dr. Solera with her. She heard the cowboy's feet pounding the earth as he approached.

"Ready," he said from behind the wall of banana leaves. They walked, partly through garden and partly through wasteland, to the garage where a truck stood in the moonlight. He got in, leaned across and opened the door for her. The hard seat was very high off the floor, and the motor made a fantastic amount of noise when he started it. Then they swung around and began to move along the driveway. As a precaution he had opened the gate when he went to get the keys. They slid through and the ranch was behind them.

He turned to her. "Have you got enough clothes on, baby? It's a lot cooler up there, you know."

Even had she known that the streets of San Felipe were going to be deep with snow, she would not have considered going back to get a coat. She looked through the windshield at the sky full of stars. "Why do you say baby?" she asked him.

He was startled. "Why do I say baby? It's the way I talk, that's all. Why, don't you like it?"

"I don't mind it," she said thoughtfully.

He did not reply. The truck roared along the highway, in and out of arroyos, through desert and brushland. At a gap between two hills he stopped and jumped out, slamming the door. After she had managed to get her door open, she too got down. He was standing in the cold at the back of the truck, looking down into the valley they had just left behind. Seeing her, he turned and began to kick the tires. "I'm paranoid about flats," he said. Far down the valley she saw the lights of a car moving along toward them.

"O.K.?" They got in, slammed the doors, and moved off. As they approached the first cantinas on the outskirts of the town, he looked briefly over at her. "You want a doctor? That means Solera."

"Yes," she said impatiently.

"But with this fiesta, I don't know. We'll have to walk." He had slowed down. Through the window, above the sound of the truck's motor, came the ceaseless rattle of firecrackers, and she could hear two or three bands playing at once.

He stopped under some tamarind trees near the empty marketplace. Men were lying at the base of the trees and in front of the dark stalls. They got out, and he locked the doors. "Come on," he said.

"Do you know where he lives?"

"Sure I know. That doesn't mean much tonight, though."

The din of marimbas, cornets, fireworks and screams came closer as they walked through the market; the crowd was at the end of the street, ahead of them. Now and then a skyrocket rushed almost horizontally to explode just above their heads.

Day was not used to seeing several thousand masked men and women shouting into one another's faces. It was clear that the fireworks were dangerous: several rockets had gone directly into the mass of people. She tried to slow their pace a bit, but he kept going until they were in the crowded plaza, under the lights and streamers, engulfed by the mob. They began to fight their way through in order to cross the square.

"Do we have to get into the middle of it?" she shouted. He seemed not to hear her, and only shoved her ahead. She felt the bodies pushing and twisting against her on all sides, saw the shiny painted masks: skulls, monkeys, demons—and the purpose of the fiesta came to her. It was not meant to celebrate the glory of God, or the saint in whose honor it was named. Instead, it was a night of collective fear, when everyone agreed to be frightened. Each person was out to scare the next; their voices were sharp with apprehensiveness. And no one knew where the skyrockets and Roman candles were going to belch their fire.

The crush had started out by being overwhelming; then it had become painful and a little unpleasant. She was sure that beneath the masks the faces were unfriendly.

In the center of the plaza was a kiosk plastered over with posters. REVINDICACIÓN, REDENCIÓN, REVOLUCIÓN, they proclaimed. She let herself be forced back into the pocket against the wall of the kiosk, where there was partial shelter from the moving throng.

"I sort of hoped we might find him here," he told her. "The important citizens are usually up there sitting with the band."

"Is he really a very bad doctor?"

"Couldn't tell you."

They stood a while watching; the uproar did not encourage conversation. But once she looked and he was not there, and her heart missed a beat. Then she began desperately to examine all the taller men nearby, thinking, He can't just have walked off without his hundred

190

dollars. When she was satisfied that he was not there, she lowered her head. Suddenly she understood that he had betrayed her to Grove. She started ahead fiercely into the crowd. I'll get to Dr. Solera by myself. She clamped her jaws together and put all her force into pushing her body forward.

Eventually she was ejected from the central core of pressure, spinning and staggering, to land against a concrete bench. A group of youths stood on top of it, peering over the heads of the multitude. As she bumped against their legs, they stared at her in surprise. One of them jumped down and stood on the ground beside her. Quickly she began in careful Spanish, "*Buenas noches.* I should like a hotel."

They started to walk. She was being buffeted so often by people rushing past that he took her arm to steady her. A skyrocket emptied its fire into a group just ahead of them, and a girl was led away sobbing, her hands over her face.

They finally left the plaza behind and walked in the small dark streets. From time to time, when the breeze shifted and blew up from across the swampland below, an evil odor filled the air—a wide, greasy stench that expanded slowly through the streets until a new wind dispersed it. The Indians sat quietly in the dust, burning candles and carbide lamps, arranging their herbs and copal in small designs on the ground in front of them, their empty eyes fixed upon a point beyond the town.

There was another plaza, smaller and deserted save for a few drunken mestizos lying on the benches and against the tree trunks. On the far side at the end of a row of humble houses was a door with a small plaque above it: PENSIÓN FÉNIX. CAMAS.

191

She stood quietly, listening to the distant excitement while he knocked. There might be no one to open the door. But then an old woman stood there, her black rebozo pulled tightly about her head, blinking and frowning at them. When the youth had spoken with her for a moment, she opened the door wider. *"A sus órdenes,"* he murmured, turning and running down the street. Day stepped inside.

There was a small patio full of furniture and plants. From there the old woman led her into a room that had nothing in it but a brass bed and a round table that held a bowl of dusty wax flowers. "Dr. Solera," she began. "Where is his house? I want to see him."

The old woman spoke for a while; Day interpreted her words as meaning that the thing would not be possible before morning. Still she insisted. She could be shown his house at least. But the old woman pulled the rebozo more firmly around her wrinkled forehead and began to mutter and sigh to herself. *"No se puede,"* she said, going out into the patio. Day followed her.

In the center was a tall cage covered with chicken wire where birds fluttered and hopped among the branches of a dead tree. The old woman stood by the cage watching the birds move in the dark, and her face assumed an expression which could have denoted satisfaction.

Day hovered in the background, waiting for a propitious moment, when the old woman might become receptive again. On a small wicker table covered with lace doilies was a frayed photograph album. She held it under the light bulb and fingered the pages. The pictures were old postcards, all of them views of a local volcano. She put the album back and took up a magazine. There were photographs of huge groups of nuns standing in rows, and a full-page portrait of the Pope. When she heard the four quick knocks on the entrance door she was absolutely certain it was Grove; it was almost as if his voice had spoken. She dropped the magazine to her side and, standing very still, looked up at the stars.

FOUR

28

IN THE GLARE of the truck's headlights the trail looked even rougher than it was; each oncoming hummock stood out sharply against the darkness behind it. Thorny drove as fast as possible, trying to keep the roar of the motor and the rattle of the chassis at a constant level. Variations in pitch and volume weakened the hypnotic power of the sound upon which, at the present moment, his thoughts depended for their sequence. Not that he believed there was any point in thinking, much less in worrying, about the mess that Grove had made. His own part in it was finished; he had done exactly as he had been told, and now once again it was merely a question of waiting, this time in doubt rather than with faith. Grove had always had the power to pull the world out from under his feet, but until now he had not done it. Trying to imagine how he would have gone about the whole thing, had he been Grove, brought him to the conclusion that everything Grove had done, from the first night on, had been done wrong.

He had telephoned Thorny at his apartment, saying he would meet him outside in the street, and there Thorny had found him, walking quickly up and down in front of the shabby entrance door, ignoring the stares of the passers-by. First he slipped Thorny a handful of grifas. They each lighted one, and started walking fast in the direction of the even poorer outskirts, past the slaughterhouse where the streets were not paved. Here there was a small park, overgrown with vegetation; at this late hour the place was completely deserted.

They sat on a bench and talked. Thorny always counted his grifas, and it was during his fourth that Grove, in his own roundabout fashion, offered Thorny a hundred thousand dollars. Grove had been smoking earlier in the evening, before coming to see him, and so Thorny assumed he was spinning one of his fantasies. He played the game for a while, and then, the talk about money having inevitably reminded him of his own precarious position, he grew morose and stared at the shadows of the leaves on the ground beside the bench.

And the little buses went past on their way through the valley to outlying villages, rattling along with their dim blue lights inside, and Thorny was thinking that there was something about being rich that made people sadistic. Grove, who was certainly very high, had gone on at such length and in such detail that he had finally cut him short. "Listen," he said. "The day I see a hundred mil I'll be down with either polio or cancer."

And Grove had cried out, "Jesus Christ! You don't know yet when I'm serious? Haven't you listened?"

They were up again, walking, with the wind swooping down out of the trees into their faces, the street lights swinging behind the leaves. Once more Grove went through the exposition of his project. At the end Thorny, although tremendously excited, shook his head. "It can't be that easy, baby. It never is."

The doubt, which he now understood had been there from the beginning, had been overshadowed by the habit of unquestioning acceptance. One day a month or so later, Grove handed him a great sheaf of typed pages. "I'm coming along on it," he told him modestly. "These are just random notes, if you want to look through them." They made the desired impression on Thorny; when he had read them he announced his willingness to collaborate on the venture. Grove did not show the surprise or pleasure he had expected. It was clear that he had counted on him from the outset.

Thorny had found it strange enough that Grove should not have observed strict secrecy in the matter; if you were going to do something like that, you went ahead and did it yourself, and said nothing to anyone. But the great question, which, had he not known Grove so well, would have put him off completely, was the size of the sum he had offered. True, it was no more than a promise, but Grove's word was good.

"I'll do it, baby. You know that," he had told Grove. "But I can't help asking myself why you don't want to save the cash and take care of it yourself."

Grove had stared at him, appalled by his lack of understanding. "What?" he cried. "Tie myself to that kind of guilt for the rest of my life? God!"

"Oh, I see," said Thorny. "You going to keep Luchita on?"

"As soon as this is fixed up I'll be able to let her go to Paris."

"I wouldn't mind a trip myself," Thorny mused. "Maybe on a freighter, the kind that takes ninety days to get to Palembang."

Grove's look had chilled all fantasy. "You'll wait a long time for that. Because you're going to live on the interest. A windfall, in a town like this?"

Thorny nodded unhappily. "You're right. God, yes!"

Now and then, at a sharp curve in the trail, the dust he was raising blew ahead and enveloped the truck, blotting out the white rocks and bushes at the sides, but he did not shift gears or slow down. At the time he had accepted Grove's explanation. It was a childish desire to feel unimplicated; very likely the handing over of

199

money would be the gesture of charity that would help him to believe in his innocence. Even accepting all this, Thorny had worried.

One time he had thought about it all night. When morning came he had telephoned Grove. In a café opposite the Correo Central he began by babbling, "I've been thinking. I don't believe I can manage it."

Grove cut him short. "Look. No matter how you picture it, it's going to turn out different. So don't picture it."

After that he was silent about his anxieties. The day they set out for Puerto Farol, Grove handed him a small box. "One now, and another every two hours." By noon he was in a state of happy indifference. As they were speeding down the eastern flank of the sierra, he said, "Nice little pills. I've got cushions all the way around."

"Good," said Grove, and was silent again. Thorny relaxed completely, happy merely to be sitting beside Grove, the one constant in a totality of flux and chaos. (Grove had remembered every detail—even, he reflected with admiration, to the playing cards.)

The bungalow was under coconut palms near the beach. Rain had discolored the dark walls, and there was the hopeless smell of mildew. "And this is the best Romero could do!" Grove snorted. "Try once to get him up off his big ass."

"But he cooperates, baby. And you've got a couch there," Thorny told him. Then he went off in the car with everything to the hotel. As he drove into the plaza he saw Romero on the steps, standing in the late-afternoon sunlight.

"*Hombre, cómo estás?*" The fraternal back-slaps, the close-up of the rotten teeth. Upstairs, in the fetid little cubicle near the bathrooms, Romero sat on the edge of the bed and spat out the pieces of toothpick he had been chewing. More imminent and insidious than the stink from the latrines was the expanding odor of Romero's sneakered feet. Following instructions, Thorny had brought up only one bottle of whiskey from the car. He took it out and poured Romero the first drink.

He ate in his room. After supper there were the cards, with Romero winning and sweating and drinking more, until his gestures were without much control, and Thorny made a show of putting the bottle on the bureau. They went on playing. One by one the guests clattered by the door to use the lavatories, returned to their rooms, and shut their doors. Then Thorny got up and went out to the latrine himself; this would give Romero the chance to take another drink. While he was out he walked softly along the balcony to the other room. The light was out. Now his heart was going too fast, and the pill was not due until twelve. On his return trip along the balcony he ran into the plants several times. Romero was in the chair with his elbows on the table when Thorny walked through the doorway, but he had taken a stiff drink; he sat with the tears coming out of his eyes, trying to keep from coughing.

Thorny took a pocket radio out of his valise, sat down, and began to move the dial. Thundershowers in the mountains made a constant crashing of static. Knowing that Romero was not going to continue the game, he sat still, waiting for him to get up and clump downstairs to bed; instead he laid his head on the table and stayed that way. Thorny sat on for a while, playing with the radio.

29

THE NOISE OF THE PALMS swishing in the dark came through the screens into the bungalow. Grove had been allowing himself to chain-smoke his grifas since eleven o'clock; he was aware of being excessively nervous, and he realized that the grifas had been a mistake. He stepped outside and stood in the sand for a moment, sniffing the still air. Then he began to walk toward the open beach ahead. The air under the trees was close and hot, but by the water there was a slight breeze stirring. It could be happening at this very moment; without being conscious of what he was doing he shut his eyes tightly and continued to walk ahead. Then he opened them. There was no one on the beach. He walked along for a way, and then turned and went back, still feeling taut and irritable. When he got to the bungalow, Thorny stood in the doorway looking out. He pushed inside past him and turned to stare at him.

"They switched rooms on us."

Grove did not answer; his mouth fell open. Then he shut it. "Where's Romero?"

"He's fine. Practically out." He gestured. "I went myself and looked. There was an old guy in there. She must have antennae. She's locked in the next room with the guy's wife."

It hit Grove like a hammer blow. She had thought of it; she was afraid. She knew him. And she was still there.

"What are you doing here?" he demanded, his voice harsh.

"I had to let you know, didn't I?"

Thorny's defensive tone infuriated him. "No! You didn't! What the bloody Christ are you down here for?"

"You want me to go in through the window?" Thorny cried. "With the other one there?"

Grove reached out and seized his shoulder roughly. "Look, Thornwald," he said, squeezing his flesh still harder. "This is your problem. You're doing it. You understand?"

He had never seen Grove's face so excessively distorted. When he felt the grip on his shoulder slowly lessen, he swung abruptly around, ran outside and got into the car.

Back at the hotel he climbed up the rickety stairs; Romero had got up from the chair and fallen onto the bed. He was snoring heavily. Thorny pushed him over against the wall and sat down on the edge of the mattress. Time began to go by, while he sat looking at the door, at the window. At one o'clock the electricity went off; he lighted a candle and watched the shadows, getting himself ready. Finally he took off his shoes and went out.

The night noises covered whatever tiny sounds he might have made climbing through the window. With the syringe in his hand he walked to the bed on the left. As he shot the curare into the fleshy neck he found his lips forming the words, "Goodbye, you old bag." (From the beginning she had disapproved of him as a friend for Grove.) There was no more motion in the bed than as if she had turned over in her sleep. He pulled the sheet up tight around her chin and went back to the window.

30

LATER, WHEN IT WAS DAYLIGHT and the old American and
his wife had left, and the servants were clattering in
the kitchen, he went in again and finished his work.
Driving back to the bungalow he felt a glow of pleasure
as he recalled the speed and precision with which he had
accomplished this last part of the venture. Grove was
waiting for him outside the bungalow, sitting on a palm
stump. They drove inland through the green world of
a banana plantation to the top of a hill behind the town,
where they stopped and watched until the fire was
brought under control. The plaza was black with people.
Then they cut through the jungle along a narrow back
trail and came out onto the coast-capital highway.

It was all done, and done in the only way possible, as
Thorny saw it, yet Grove was not content; he was fret-
ting about the American girl. Over and over he said he
would never be sure what she had seen. She had gone
on her way quietly, yes, but how could he know she
hadn't happened onto the truth (it must have been
fairly evident, if for any reason she had really looked),
and rather than see herself getting involved, had merely
shut the door and gone away, free to tell everything
later?

"That's got to be changed," Grove said with finality.

"It's a little late in the day to change anything,"
Thorny told him, stung to realize that Grove did not
consider his work a brilliant success.

Grove said nothing. As they rounded a curve, Thorny
stole a glance at him, and decided that he had been

shut out. Grove was going to do something crazy, and without taking him into his confidence.

Even so, he could scarcely believe Grove was serious when, two days later after getting him down to Los Hermanos, he expounded the outrageous new project to him.

"You *want* trouble, don't you?" he said slowly. "Have you got to walk another tightrope now, when everything's all right?"

"The answer is yes," Grove snapped. "You'll be stuck here for a few days, that's all. They're coming down tonight."

He did not ask Grove why the girl never appeared. Three mornings later, after they had managed to calm the old man somewhat, Grove remarked, "It's a good thing she's responsive to treatment. If she were anything like him, Paloma'd never be able to manage her."

Forbearing to criticize, since criticism was useless, Thorny merely said, "The old guy's a handful." He would not have thought Grove capable of such protracted nonsense. Instead of living a normal life, waiting quietly for word from London and Montreal, he was hysterically involved in a round-the-clock game with two American tourists: feeding them LSD, shooting them full of scopolamine and morphine, putting them under and bringing them out again, and providing special sound effects for each phase of the program. (This preoccupation with the tape recorders struck him as the most infantile bit of all. The room at Los Hermanos had to be kept dark, and at times there was an endless whispering, scarcely loud enough to hear unless he remained in there purposely to listen; then the repeated phrases seemed to grow in volume and fill every corner.)

That period had been a strain; Thorny and Dirk

worked in four-hour shifts. The schedule had to be observed with absolute precision. Each day Grove made three round trips up to the capital; on arriving back at Los Hermanos he was often short-tempered.

"Anyway," Thorny said, the morning they drove to the station and he helped Grove carry the old man onto the train for San Felipe, "whatever happens now, we've done everything we could." He knew better than to say, I've done everything. But Grove turned on him with irritation.

"What is this always about things happening?" he demanded. "Things don't happen. It depends on who comes along."

"You're right," he agreed, and he recalled the remark shortly afterward at the ranch. Grove had telephoned him the following day, saying he needed him; when he arrived he was waiting for him in the little library off his own bedroom. He got up and shut the door.

"You'll eat in here," he told him. "Your job is to tune in on all conversations, whatever room we're in, and tape everything. She's not being honest with me."

"I thought you said she was responsive," said Thorny, trying not to grin.

"That doesn't mean she's being honest now."

Thorny listened before, during, and after mealtimes, and was impressed. There was no doubt that neither of them remembered anything at all about Puerto Farol; they were convinced that they had first met Grove down there at the dock.

"There's something she's holding back," Grove complained, after he had studied the recordings.

"Get her mad if you can. Catch her off guard," Thorny advised.

"She's going to give me trouble yet."

With that in his mind, Grove could be counted on to react badly to the news about the bonfire; with misgivings Thorny went in to tell him. Earlier in the day Grove had handed him a pile of papers to burn, most of them typewritten notes of the sort he was always making. He would not have bothered to call it to Grove's attention had he not seen the girl wandering around out there in the garden, near the spot where he had burned them. When she had gone in, he left his hammock in the bamboo brake and walked over to check. One of the servants, before going off to the fiesta, must have spilled water on the fire, he decided, for the papers had not burned completely. He picked up those that remained and carried them into the kitchen, pinching off the charred edges on the way. At the sink he washed his hands, and while he dried them he glanced over the top fragment.

fer
as scaffolding f
(Note: for therap
rd day—tape of beach at La Lib
h "Dawn will be breaking soon."
nto RED notebook a

It went on in this way; there was not even another complete sentence—only bits of phrases and truncated words. However, there was nothing to do but take the stuff in and report what had happened.

"What?" Grove sprang up out of his chair, grabbed the papers.

Thorny was silent. He heard the steady spray of a

sprinkler in the courtyard rattling as it hit the big banana leaves. After a lapse, Grove said, looking fixedly at him, "This makes it bad."

"For Christ's sake! She just walked past!"

Grove still glared at him. He raised his voice, "Believe me when I say it's bad."

"I believe you." Thorny moved toward the door.

"Stay here," said Grove sharply, beginning to walk around the center of the room. Then for nearly ten minutes he talked without stopping. Finally he threw himself onto the divan and stretched out at full length. "It's as though I'd known all along it was going to be this way. Unbelievable how things can dovetail."

Thorny looked at the floor. "It depends on who comes along. Isn't that what you said?"

Grove's glance was cold. "I'm as much against it as you are. It's just where the whole thing is now. You can see that."

"You know what you're doing."

It was not much later when Thorny went out into the courtyard and saw the girl standing on the rocks down below; quickly Grove brought an immersion heater and made the doctor his tea.

A good while after dark, while Grove and the girl were in the kitchen, Thorny went down and got Pablo, who had stayed on at the generator. ("There's a señor who's sick, and I have to take him to San Felipe.") Together they carried the old man from the bed to the truck. Thorny got in and shut the door. Then he drove off alone in the dark, down the trail that ultimately led to Barrancas, until he got to the dangerous stretch edging the cliff. If there was even a mule coming along here, you had to stop the car. In the daytime, far below, you could see the round tops of the big trees down there. He had to do the rest alone, but even so, it did not take more than two minutes. Then he went on down a mile or so until he came to a place where he could turn the car.

No one ever went down into that part of the country; it was empty land. Scrub mimosa and cactus at the foot of the cliff, and then terrible formless thickets of thorned bramble, like rolls of barbed wire. And still lower, the tufted forest of high green trees. And nothing lasted long down there, in any case, he thought, glancing out over the vast moonlit lands below: the buzzards, flopping and tugging, and the ants hurrying in endless lines, night and day.

"Why don't you go to bed?" Grove asked him when he got back.

"Yeah," he said, and went down to see Pablo at the generator. Earlier they had made some grifas together. Now they sat smoking in the moonlight, listening to the radio. Before he relaxed completely, for he had no idea how long he might stay down there with Pablo, he made himself stand up and go over to the truck: he had left the keys in the ignition. He was almost down to the generator again when Pablo called out, and it was a shock to find the girl standing there; he had imagined she would be with Grove. The only thing possible was to go up to the house for a consultation.

Grove's face grew nasty when Thorny told him. "Oh, she wants it to be at San Felipe, does she? O.K., take her. It's perfect!" Then he explained, and told Thorny exactly what to do.

"You're out of your bloody mind!" said Thorny, in spite of himself.

Grove smiled broadly. "I'll give you ten minutes' start."

Bravado, thought Thorny, tramping back down to the generator. It was dangerous enough anyway, without

209

the acrobatics. He stopped for a moment beside a high cactus and finished off a partly smoked grifa from his pocket.

He was very high driving up to San Felipe, and the girl had decided to be hostile. The confusion of the alameda, the fireworks and the yelling, made him even more nervous. When he had spotted Grove and knew Grove had seen him and the girl, he pushed into the crowd, looking straight ahead, and fought his way through to the open. Quickly he passed between the rows of silent seated Indians, and into the dark street where he had parked.

FIVE

31

THE OLD WOMAN'S FACE lost its contented look; turning her head away from the birdcage, she frowned, and then shuffled across to the door. And there he was in a white sweater, suave and gleaming. Day watched him take the old woman's measure and alter his personality to fit the need. He assumed a courteous, almost deferential air, and said a few gentle phrases to her; then he stepped past her into the patio. Grinning at Day across the birdcage, he began to talk very fast.

"'I admit I was crazy about the dame,' the suspect told police after the six-hour grilling. 'I followed her everywhere. I wanted to know what made her tick. But that don't make me the killer.'"

If only he really were mad, she thought, his behavior would be less frightening. As she did not reply, but merely stood staring at him, he went on. "In the next edition they print the full confession. What are you doing here?" The insolent tone of his final words reawakened her anger.

"I'm sleeping here," she said without expression. The night was growing colder.

The old woman still stood holding the door ajar, watching Grove with an admiration only faintly tempered by mistrust. He was so clearly a young lover; it was so natural of him to come and try to persuade the girl to go out into the fiesta. She called over to her: "Ándale, guapa! Salga un poco con su novio." It was ridiculous enough, but Day could not laugh.

Grove stepped around the cage to her and touched

213

her arm. "It was just what I thought. He felt like going outside for some air. He took a walk."

She wanted passionately to believe him; it was difficult, and she may have allowed her doubt to show. "All right," he said, giving her an ugly smile. "He's been kidnaped and probably murdered. Is that better?"

Ignoring the irony, agreeing to accept the story, she went on. "Does he seem like himself?"

"More like himself than anybody else, anyway," he said with impatience. "Why don't we go up the street for a drink? Then you come back and sleep here, and in the morning I'll get Solera and bring him around and pick you up. That's what you want, isn't it? Isn't that why you came to San Felipe?"

She considered him a moment. He still thinks he can manipulate me, she thought scornfully—as if anything could change the way she felt about him. He expects me to put up resistance. An unexpected compliance could throw him off balance, and she might seize the initiative in the battle. The fact that she was unable to conceive of their relationship in any other terms rather frightened her, but above all she was infuriated by being forced to engage in such a struggle.

The sputter of firecrackers and the barking of dogs never had subsided for an instant. The old woman still stood there, her hand on the door, watching them, perfectly certain that at a given moment the girl would capitulate. And sure enough, presently she moved listlessly around the birdcage, dragging the back of her hand across the meshes of chicken wire to make a rasping noise, and came walking over toward the door. The young man followed quickly, smiled at the old woman, and gently pushed the girl outside. She nodded

214

as he passed in front of her. "*Claro. Una noche de fiesta
. . .*" She shut the door.

The stars burned in the cold sky. They walked
briskly through the deserted streets, with the noise of
the fiesta behind them. On the outskirts of the town
there was a rocky eminence, high above the wasteland.
Tall trees stood near the edge. The squat adobe building in front of them looked very small. Music came
through the open door.

"It'll be good tonight," he said.

The crimson and orange glow of a jukebox was the
only light in the main room. Tables were grouped
around the instrument; a dozen mestizos sat in a state
of torpor.

Behind the café was an open garden planted with
high pines. The bamboo pavilions among the trees were
scarcely lit. People sat everywhere, and bands of children raced through the gloom tossing firecrackers that
exploded among the cactuses. Only when Grove had
taken her all the way across the garden did she understand why a café had been built in this particular spot.
The place was at the very end of the town; the back of
its garden skirted the promontory. Along the curve of
the parapet were more of the bamboo huts, with slivers
of pale light spilling through the slits in their walls.
Down to the lower end of the garden he led her, and
they went into a booth. There was only one small bench;
they sat side by side looking out across the lightless
landscape beyond the railing. An Indian waiter wearing
felt bedroom slippers appeared in the doorway. Grove
ordered *habanero;* there was only beer.

She wished the night were over. Ironically she was
reminded of the sentence from her dream. If only dawn

215

were going to be breaking soon, and there were not the bare little room and the hours in the hard bed to look forward to before meeting Dr. Solera. The dry soughing of the wind when it passed now and then through the pines made the minutes seem much longer.

After a while the Indian came back, bringing a pail of ice with two bottles of beer in it. He left an opener on the table and went away.

The moon had moved in the sky; down there she could detect certain remote shadowy canyons that had not been visible a while ago. As she sat letting her eyes follow their faint contours, she thought of the terrible expression she had caught on Grove's face in the kitchen, and it seemed to her that all the forces which had made this present scene inevitable had come into being at that time, and that nothing had changed since then.

He sat first in one position and then in another, although the bench was not noticeably uncomfortable. Twice he rose and stood with his glass in his hand, looking silently over the railing into the dark.

A family group filed across the garden and out with a great noise of laughter and chatter. Then in a nearby booth a powerful salute was detonated. There were screams, and the women cried, "*Ay, Dios!*"

Finally she said, "I've got to go back. I'm half dead with the cold." Her voice sounded to her as though it were coming over an amplifier—an unreal, husky, intimate whisper.

Somewhere back in the garden another large firecracker exploded. Several strings of small ones were tossed over the cliff, crackling and flaming.

Without getting up, he leaned over the railing and looked downward. There was only the darkness there, and she knew it as well as he, yet she too found herself

216

staring out at the same part of the invisible countryside. For an instant there was enough silence in the garden behind her for her to hear the tiny, far-off sound of a baying dog.

Presently he said, "Look, Day." She waited for him to go on, and since he did not, she turned her head toward him. His hand, resting on his thigh, held a large black revolver.

SIX

32

Steering the truck through the gate, Thorny wondered whether Pablo would still be awake. It occurred to him that there was no one at all in the house. No servants, no guests, no hosts—only the wind in the courtyard, rustling the leaves.

The light over the generator was on, and Pablo sat on the ground listening to the radio. He dropped down beside him and squinted, so that Pablo got to his feet and snapped off the light. Squatting again, now in the precise moonlight, the boy tossed Thorny a grifa.

"*Pobrecita!* She wanted to see her husband in the hospital?"

"Yes. Shut the motor off. There's nobody in the house."

They had smoked until shortly after daybreak. When Thorny wandered up to bed, the courtyard looked haggard in the pale new light; the air in his room was hot. There was a cricket singing somewhere behind the curtains. After he had bolted the heavy door he walked across and let the blinds fall with a crash. From his pillow he listened to the cricket repeat its one small glassy note, again and again.

At two o'clock there was a banging on the door. He groaned, "Oh, Christ!" got up, and opened it.

Grove stood there with a thermos of coffee, the bright sunlight shining on the leaves behind him. "Let's get going," he said. "You're driving."

On the way up to the capital they did not talk. The long reaches of the desperate outer slums were pink in the sunset as the convertible rolled down into the city.

"Luchita took off for Paris this morning," Grove said suddenly. "She phoned from the airport."

Thorny made a noise in his throat.

They stood on the terrace of Grove's apartment, drinking very cold beer, looking at the decaying light in the western sky. "When can we expect a change?" Thorny asked, without having known, an instant before, that he was going to say anything.

"It'll be coming through. Your credit's good until then. Up to a point."

"Up to a hundred thousand." Thorny's voice had absolutely no inflection.

Grove turned on him. "Go on home, will you?" he snapped, his face savage and ready for tears, like a small boy's.

"Christ almighty!" Thorny set his glass down on the table with a bang and went into the *sala*. Grove's voice was shouting after him. He stood still, waiting for it to suggest that his work had not been essential, did not deserve to be paid for.

"I said up to a certain point!" Grove appeared in the doorway, black and faceless against the dying sky. "Make sense. How can you have it until I get it?"

But an unfamiliar accent of confusion in his voice had struck Thorny's ears; he watched Grove come into the room toward him, and it seemed the right moment to move for the establishment of a new status. Not to have to pay for meals, to come home and lie down in a really comfortable bed; that was all he had in his mind at the time. He turned and went out into the foyer, stood looking into the blue bedroom where he had slept the night they had come back from Puerto Farol. "My room," he thought, and he walked in, took off his jacket and shoes, and threw himself down on the bed. His hands cupped behind his head, he lay a while staring dreamily at the ceiling, waiting to see; Grove knew he was still there.

A little later he heard Grove go out. He got up, stretching, went and turned on the hot water in the bathtub. While he waited for it to fill, he wandered out into the kitchen and told Manuel and Paloma to serve his dinner at half past eight. Walking slowly back to the bedroom along the terrace, he stopped a moment to examine the pools and fountains on the way; it was the first time he had ever really looked at them.

In the bathroom he turned off the roaring water, seized a big turkish towel, and wiped the steam from the enormous mirror on the wall; it had a wide beveled edge that played tricks with the image. He ducked his head back and forth a few times, watching his face change. Then he moistened a grifa, lit it, and partially undressed. Taking a pair of curved scissors from the cabinet, he began to cut his fingernails.